THE MYSTERY OF THE CUPBOARD

OTHER MORROW JUNIOR BOOKS BY
LYNNE REID BANKS

The Adventures of King Midas
The Magic Hare
One More River

AVAILABLE FROM OTHER PUBLISHERS

The Indian in the Cupboard
The Return of the Indian
The Secret of the Indian

The Fairy Rebel
The Farthest-Away Mountain
I, Houdini
Melusine: A Mystery

THE

MYSTERY OF THE CUPBOARD

LYNNE REID BANKS

ILLUSTRATED BY

TOM NEWSOM

Morrow Junior Books
New York

1 2 3 4 5 6 7 8 9 10

Library of Congress Cataloging-in-Publication Data
Reid Banks, Lynne.   The mystery of the cupboard / by Lynne Reid Banks ;
illustrated by Tom Newsom.   p. cm.   Summary: After the family moves
to the country to a house recently inherited by his mother, Omri finds many
secrets revealed to him when he accidently discovers the link between the house
and the magic cupboard. Sequel to "The Secret of the Indian."
ISBN 0-688-12138-1.—ISBN 0-688-12635-9 (lib. bdg.)
[1. Family life—Fiction.   2. Magic—Fiction.   3. Toys—Fiction.   4. Moving,
Household—Fiction.]   I. Newsom, Tom, ill.   II. Title.
PZ7.R2737My 1993 [Fic]—dc20 92-39295 CIP AC

To Adiel, Gillon, and Omri,
sine qua non.
And to Betsy Hass.

Contents

THE MYSTERY OF THE CUPBOARD

ONE

The Longhouse

"But Mum, I don't want to move house again!"

Omri's mother stared at him with her mouth slightly ajar. She turned away for a moment as if she simply couldn't think of a thing to say, and then swiftly turned back.

"Omri, you know what, you're incredible. Ever since we moved here you've done nothing but moan. You hated the district, you hated the street, you hated the house—"

"I never said I hated the house! I like the house. I love the garden. Anyway, even if I did hate it, I wouldn't want to move. All that packing and general hassle last time, it was awful! Why do we have to move *again*?"

"Listen, darling. You remember the freak storm?"

Omri stared at her. Remember it? Could anyone who'd survived it possibly ever forget it?

"Stupid me, of course you do, I only meant— well, it wrecked the greenhouse—"

"It wrecked *my room*—"

"The chimney fell off, the roof had to be—"

"But Mum, that was all months ago. It's all been mended, pretty well."

"At vast cost," put in his father, who was sitting at the breakfast-room table writing out a description of their house. It was coming home unexpectedly early and catching his father on the phone to an estate agent that had tipped Omri off that his parents were thinking about selling and moving.

"Yes, and now with a new roof and everything, it's a good time to sell. Besides, Dad really hates living in town."

Now it was Omri's turn to have his mouth hang open.

"You mean we're not going to live in London?"

"No. We're going to live in the country."

Omri sat up sharply. "The *country*!" he almost shouted, as dismayed as if his father had announced they were going to live at the bottom of the sea.

"Yes, dear, the country," said his mother. "That big green place with all the trees—you know, you've seen it through the car window when we've been racing from one hideous town to another."

Omri ignored her sarcasm. "Would it be Kent?" His best friend, Patrick, lived in Kent.

"No."

That put the lid on any thoughts that it might not be so bad.

"But—but—are we just moving because of Dad?"

"Certainly not," his father said promptly. "We're also moving because the local high school, which your brothers already go to and which you will, in theory, be starting at in September, is a sink. It's enough that two of my sons come home two days out of five looking as if they've fallen under a bus. It's enough that Gillon's marks are in steady decline. I'm not going to compound my mistake by sending *you* there too."

But Omri had stopped listening and was halfway to the door.

"Do Adiel and Gillon know?"

"We were going to have a family conference tonight after supper. Only you wrung it out of me," said his father. "And you don't have to go telling them straight away—"

But Omri was already charging up the stairs. At the top he burst into the first room he came to, which was Gillon's.

"We're going to live in the country!" he exploded.

Gillon, who had jumped up guiltily from his bed

(where he'd been lying reading a magazine instead of doing homework) because he thought it was a parent, slumped back again and stared at Omri, stunned.

"The country!" he repeated in exactly the same tone as Omri had used. "We can't be! What'll we do there? There's nothing to do in the country, we'll be bored out of our minds!"

But Omri had already vanished and was beating on Adiel's door. Adiel really was doing homework, and had locked his door to keep out intruders.

"Get lost!" he yelled from his desk.

"Ad, listen! Dad's just told me. We're going to live in the country!"

There was a pause, then the bolt was drawn, the door opened, and Adiel's face appeared. He stared at Omri in silence for a few seconds.

"Good," he said maddeningly, and shut the door in his face.

"Are you crazy?" Omri called through the door. Gillon had come out and was standing next to him.

"He said 'good'!" Omri told him indignantly.

"Ask him if he's crazy."

"I just have!"

"Are you crazy?" Gillon shouted through the door at the top of his voice.

"Boys, stop that row, that's enough! Come down and we'll talk about it!" came their father's irritated voice from the foot of the stairs.

Omri and Gillon trailed down and back into the breakfast room. After a few minutes, Adiel, looking studiedly unconcerned, joined them.

"Now then. Listen first, *then* blow your tops, okay? This house, due to a fluke in the housing market, is suddenly worth a lot of money."

"How much?" said Gillon, for whom money was the most important thing in life.

"A lot more than what we paid for it. Just because it's in London and lots of people, whom I can only regard as totally insane, want to live in London."

"And at the precise moment when we were thinking of selling anyway," put in their mother eagerly, "something really wonderful has happened. I've inherited a lovely house."

"Inherited? Does that mean we get it for nothing?"

"Yes! Isn't it incredible?"

"But what's it like? Have you seen it?"

"Well, er—no, not yet. But it sounds beautiful. Not as big as this one—"

"WHAT!" all the boys—even Adiel—yelled in chorus.

"But that won't matter," put in their father quickly, "because we will not be surrounded on all sides by this stinking, overcrowded, crime-ridden city where you can't snatch a breath of clean air or walk ten yards without being mugged—"

"Lionel, there's no need to exaggerate, none of us has ever been mugged—"

"—Or at least tripping over litter, and we will live in peace and safety and beauty, in a much nicer, if *somewhat* smaller, house with much more land, and we'll have a better life. Now what on this polluted earth, may I ask, is wrong with that?"

Silence. Then Adiel said, "Sounds okay to me. Only where would we go to school?"

Their father and mother gave each other a little married look. Their father cleared his throat and said, "Well. What would you say to boarding?"

He was looking only at Adiel when he said it, and Adiel didn't flinch. But Gillon gave a great screech and fell off his chair onto the floor, where he lay spread-eagled and twitching.

"Oh, get up," said his mother, hauling on one arm. "You clown. He didn't mean you."

Gillon sat up sharply.

"He didn't? Why not? Aren't I good enough to go to boarding school?"

"No," said Adiel. "At boarding school you're not only expected to work, you have to keep your room tidy. You'd be kicked out in a week."

Gillon uttered a short word under his breath and slumped back onto the floor. From there he said, "I suppose we couldn't have a dog."

"A dog!" exclaimed Omri. "What about Kitsa?" Kitsa was his cat.

"It would eat her," said Gillon cheerfully. "Bit of a laugh, eh?" He sat up again. "It'd be good, we might get a rottweiler and then it would eat you too."

"What we might actually get," remarked their mother, "is a pony."

The boys all looked at one another in bewilderment. None of them had ever shown the faintest interest in riding. Only for Omri did the idea of a horse have any associations. But they were very pleasant ones.

He said slowly, "That might be all right. I wouldn't mind that."

"Are you crazy? You've never even sat on a horse!" said Gillon.

"I'd like to, though," said Omri.

His vision of "the country" as a barren wilderness devoid of all entertainment blurred a little, and out of the mist rode a familiar figure: an American Indian, seated astride a strong, alert brown pony, with his hand raised in stern greeting. He cocked one buckskin-clad leg over the pony's neck and slid to the ground, where he stood knee-deep in lush English grass. What was odd was, in Omri's vision, he was the same size as Omri—well, bigger, obviously, because he was a man. The odd thing about this was that Omri had only ever seen him small. But often in Omri's night- and daydreams, he appeared full-size.

Now, in the daydream, the Indian made a stirrup of both hands and gestured with his head. Without hesitating, Omri ran up to him, put his left foot in the hands and felt himself lifted. A moment later he was on the pony's warm back.

It felt terrific. He looked down at his Indian— his friend—and the Indian narrowed his black eyes at him approvingly and gestured with both fists. Omri understood him instantly and echoed that squeezing movement with his legs. The pony started forward. . . .

"What are you grinning at?" asked Adiel, who was watching him. "You've got your loopy look."

Omri hastily banished Little Bear from his mind and rearranged his face into solemn lines. "Nothing, I was just thinking. And where would me and Gillon go to school?"

"*Gillon and I,*" corrected his father between his teeth for the three thousandth time. "Locally. We're looking into it now."

It'll be some tinny little country school with eight pupils," said Gillon.

"Oh, come on, boys, cheer up. It won't happen till the summer at the very earliest. And meanwhile there's all the fun of going to see our new place. We're going this weekend."

"Is it by the sea?"

"Not far—about six miles."

Gillon scrambled up. His eyes were on Omri. In them, Omri discerned a brotherly signal: *Might not be so bad, what d'you think?* Omri gave an almost imperceptible nod. His heart felt suddenly, unaccountably light.

Visiting the new house was quite a lot of fun, apart from the long car journey, which was obviously hard to take, especially as their parents had recently gone on a health kick and flatly refused to take them to motorway service stops where they insisted you could only buy junk food. They had to wait till they were off the motorway, by which time the pubs had stopped serving lunch and the next meal would be tea. However, by the time they found a tea place they were *all* so hungry that health was forgotten and they stuffed themselves with tea cakes and scones and thick cream and strawberry jam and flapjacks till they nearly burst. They might as well have had the hamburger-and-chips meal in the first place.

On the way again, Omri asked, "Who did you inherit this house from?"

"Some cousin I never knew existed. An old, old man who died recently without leaving a will. It seems I'm his nearest relative. The lawyers contacted me and said I was to have the house. Bit of luck, eh?"

"Let's wait till we've seen it," said Gillon, never one to see the bright side until he was forced to.

The house was outside a village in deepest Dorset. It took four hours to get there, and find it.

After passing through a mysterious, dark tunnel, they drew up at last beside a big gate in a lane. There was no sign of the house, which was screened from the road by a high hedge of mixed wild trees and shrubs, not like London hedges, which tended all to be made of the same thing.

They entered through another gate, a small one, and went up a path. The first thing that struck them was how incredibly different it all was from London. The boys could hardly grasp the fact that they were actually going to live in a place like this, surrounded by open countryside, with no other houses in sight. They felt weird about it, as if they were on another planet.

The details in the lawyers' letter had talked about "an acre of land, outbuildings, a paddock, and a small wood running down to a river that borders the property." They stood on the overgrown lawn and stared around them in wonderment. In the distance were rounded hills, some with trees crowning them, and nearer were sloping fields. It was indeed "a big green place with lots of trees."

"We're in the Hidden Valley," murmured their mother. "Isn't it absolutely magical?"

"How much of all this is ours?" asked Gillon.

"Just this bit, stupid," said Adiel. "Up to the fence."

"No," said their mother, consulting a sort of map the lawyers had sent. "More than that. That big field is ours—that's the paddock. Down to those trees down there. That's the river. And there's more across the lane."

"*More?*" The garden at home, which they had considered vast, dwindled by comparison to tablecloth-size.

Their mother led them across the lane to the big gate. Beyond it was a kind of yard with buildings on three sides. One was a big workshop, and their father headed for that like an arrow. Another was three open bays under a corrugated iron roof. A third looked like an old barn and had several doors.

"That's the pigsty and stable," their mother said. "Long disused. And a couple of rooms for feed and stuff. And somewhere there are henhouses."

"Long disused too, I suppose," said Adiel.

"No, as a matter of fact, there are hens. Some old party from the village has been coming in to look after them occasionally and collect the eggs. It should be around the back there somewhere."

The boys belted around behind the pigsty and found about a dozen hens, one of them with five tiny chicks running around squeaking. There was a handsome cockerel too, who obliged with a regal crow as soon as they appeared.

"Hey, check this out, Dad!" called Adiel, bending over a long box. "Fresh eggs!" He emerged holding two in each hand.

"And fresh chicken!" said Gillon.

"If you can kill them," said their mother.

"Anyone would kill a chicken to get a roast one," said Gillon, who'd never killed anything in his life.

"Well, never mind the livestock now. Let's go and look over the house!" said their mother excitedly. "My very own house! I can't wait!"

The two-story house was made of stone, with a thatched roof. It was a funny shape, long and thin, with a sort of bend or wave in the middle.

"It's a real Dorset longhouse!" enthused their father.

"A *longhouse!*" Omri almost shouted.

They all looked at him curiously.

"Yes . . . That's what these long one-room-deep stone houses are called around here."

The rooms were fairly small, but there were eight main ones altogether—four bedrooms in a row and four little linked living rooms. No corridors. Two flights of stairs, one on each end, so the two middle bedrooms led off the two outer ones. The bathroom had been added in modern times, built out at the back over the kitchen. From every window there were beautiful views.

The garden was neglected and the thatched roof gave Omri's father pause.

"It's all very well," he said, while they all rushed about getting enthusiastic. "I love the place, it's perfect, that workshop! My dream of a studio! But have you any idea what it costs to rethatch a thatched roof? And we'll have to, almost right away. Look, it's rotten." He reached out through one of the tiny windows upstairs and pulled a handful of thatch out of the deep eaves. It was black with age and damp and it had a musty smell.

From below, Omri called in an odd tone, "Come and see this!"

The others went outside and around to the gable end of the house, nearest the road. Up under the sloping thatch was a plaque, inset into the stone. It was engraved in very worn old-fashioned writing. Omri couldn't read it, but their mother, with difficulty, made it out.

Blessed the man
who fearing God
buildeth for
posterity. LB. 1704

When she'd finished reading, they all stood for a moment. Then Gillon said, "What's posterity?"

"It means your bottom," said Adiel.

The older two burst out laughing. Only Omri didn't—he wasn't listening.

"Don't be fatuous, boys," said their father. "Not 'posterior'! For posterity means 'for those who'll come after you.' "

Gillon and Adiel were still choking down their mirth when Omri said quietly, "We're definitely going to like living here." They all looked at him.

"How do you know?" said Gillon with a bit of jeer in his voice.

"It's a longhouse," said Omri mysteriously. "And—LB."

"What?"

"Someone with the initials LB built this house."

"Big deal. So what?" ·

"LB's are lucky for me," said Omri quietly.

T W O

Kitsa Goes Missing

They moved in August.

It hadn't been so hard, after all, to leave the old house on Hovel Road. Omri had secretly been quite glad to, in the end. After all, his room had been totally wrecked by the Big Storm. For months he'd slept on a mattress on the floor, and done his homework at an ordinary old table, and thought about all his things that the storm had demolished or blown away. His market-bought chest had been destroyed, along with his Japanese table, his desk, his collections, and all his other stuff, his links with childhood. It was time for a new start.

"Dad," he asked at one stage when they were packing up, "will you have the same bank?"

"A different branch, but yes," said his father, puzzled. But then he understood. "Ah, your mysterious package that you asked me to have them put in their vaults. Don't worry, Omri. They'll keep it safe."

"But will they move it to the bank near our new house?" Omri persisted anxiously.

"I'll make sure they do," said his father.

Omri wrote to Patrick, his friend and the sharer of his greatest secret, on the day before moving day.

> *Dear Patrick,*
>
> *We're moving to the country tomorrow. Wish it was near you but it's the other way. We'll be farther apart than ever. I'll write the new address at the end. Keep in touch.*
>
> *Dad says IT will come to the new place with us, to the new bank. I hope you're keeping Boone safe. I'm taking Little Bear and Bright Stars with me, and Matron and Fickits. I mean I'm carrying them. I'll find somewhere safe for them in my new room. I just wanted you to know. I'm taking all my other plastic figures too. Not that we'll do anything about them.*
>
> *Hope you're okay and that your mum has planted a new orchard after the storm. You must come and visit us in the new*

house. It's quite fun, lots of old barns and stuff, and there's hens that the last owner (he died, he was very old, Mum says he was my removed cousin or something) left. Their eggs have very orange yolks, like almost red. A neighbor's been looking after them and Dad wants to keep them. And there's a wood and a river and the sea quite close. And Mum says we might have a pony!!

Bye. Omri.

P.S. I'm dreading starting at a new school. It's the local comp, of course. I went to meet the head, it's a woman. She's an improvement on Mr. Johnson anyhow. Her name's Mrs. Everest. She wears a wig that looks just like a big tea cozy.

Two days after the move—two frantic, chaotic days, which followed a frantic, chaotic fortnight packing up—Omri was standing out in the lane that ran alongside their longhouse.

Both his parents and his brothers were indoors trying to make some kind of order in the various rooms, which were still so jammed with a mass of unsorted furniture and crates that you could hardly move around.

The reason Omri wasn't with them was because he was desperately hunting for Kitsa.

She had come from London in the moving van, in a cat basket. Too near to this (as it turned out) had been a large silk lampshade. When they arrived, the lampshade was found in shreds, ripped by Kitsa's resentful claws, reached through the bars of the cat basket.

The moment Omri had let her out, his mother, who was at the end of her rope, shouted at her, "You wicked animal, you've ruined my best lamp!" and made a swipe at her. Kitsa had fled, and Omri hadn't seen her since.

"She'll be back," his mother—who, when things calmed down, felt awful about her—tried to comfort him. But he was frantic with worry. How could she find her way back when she didn't know this was now her home?

He had already searched the whole property: the henhouse, the pigsty, the workshop, the barn, as well as the paddock and the wood, which ran down to a little river. He'd called her till he was hoarse.

He was miserable, absolutely miserable. Nobody could cheer him up, though even Gillon tried.

"She'll come back," he said. "She's just giving us a hammering because we moved her."

Now as Omri stood in the lane and called her, without much hope, up the lane came, not Kitsa, alas, but a red postal van, which stopped at their gate. The postman leaned out.

"Mistle Hay Farmhouse?" he asked.

Omri said it was.

"Long time since there were any post for here," he said. "You moved in I 'spect, bin empty a good while and the old man never got no letters to speak of, real recluse he was. Well, this be for you by looks of it, kid's writin'." And he handed Omri a letter. It was addressed to him, and it was from Patrick. Omri read it at once, standing in the lane.

Dear Omri,

Thanks for the letter. I looked on the map. Blimey, you're a long way off. Too bad. Don't know when we'll get a chance to meet. I'll work on my mum to go on holiday near you but I bet she won't, she likes going over to Calais on the ferry to shop every chance she gets. Dead boring except the boat trip. She spends every minute in the French supermarket buying stuff we can easily get in Safeways at home. Crazy.

I've been thinking. I wish you hadn't put IT in the bank. I know why you did, but still. Every time I look at Boone, I get lonely for him and wonder how he's getting on. I sometimes imagine I'm in Texas, or that Boone comes back here and I talk to him.

Don't laugh YOU PILLOCK. I bet you feel the same about Little Bear.

Guess what, my aunt came to visit and brought Emma. (Tamsin was at summer ski-camp—yea!) It was great. We talked and talked about Them. She'd brought Ruby Lou and we played with them and pretended they were alive, only we had to stop cos Em started crying. She's okay though really. She said the same as me, that she wished you hadn't put IT in the bank. She said you should have asked us first.

You couldn't change your mind, could you?

Good luck with your new school and the Tea Cozy. Maybe she's bald underneath it. You'll have to try to make it fall off and see. My school's a real toilet.

See ya.
Patrick.

P.S. Em and Tamsin are still at the old school. Em told me Mr. Johnson fell off his bicycle into some prickly bushes. She says he's never been the same since the day of the storm. Keeps talking to himself, there's a rumor he's gone a bit irregular (that's our school slang for barmy).

This letter at least took Omri's mind off Kitsa for a while. After reading it, he went up to his room.

He'd chosen one of the "inner" bedrooms so that he would be the one who had to pass through Gillon's room to get to the stairs, and not the other way around. It was not a perfect arrangement, but better than Gillon having right-of-way through *his* room. He'd made Gillon—who had been desperate for the outside bedroom—promise always to knock, if he did need to come in, which was unlikely. Omri was a very private person. He planned to put a bolt on, like his old room had.

His new bed was up, and his new desk. They were both pinewood. He decided to put up loads of shelves, or rather ask his dad to. His dad, however, was overwhelmed with work.

"Time you learned to put up shelves for yourself," he'd said shortly, on Day One.

"Okay! Can I borrow your drill?"

"No."

"So how can I—"

"Oh, I'll do it eventually! Give me a chance, I'm up to my neck!"

Meanwhile, Omri made do with some planks he found—that was one great thing about this place, there was so much junk lying about—laid across piles of bricks. He cleaned them all first and the shelves looked quite good. Since losing all his stuff in the storm he'd collected a few new books and some other bits and pieces, and these he arranged on the new shelves.

He looked at the top shelf and thought how good IT would look, standing right in the middle, with its new coat of white paint and new mirror in the door. . . .

No. He mustn't be tempted. He'd made up his mind. No more of that. He'd promised himself. He must stick to what he'd decided. He fingered a small neat parcel in his jeans pocket. Where to put it? Where would be a really safe place?

"Ah!" he exclaimed aloud.

He took four more bricks, and turned them so the indented sides faced each other. Then he opened the packet, put Little Bear and Bright Stars and the baby, and the pony, between two of the bricks, lying down in the little hollow, and on the other side, between the other two bricks, he laid Sergeant Fickits and Matron. He felt there was something faintly scandalous about them lying side by side like that, but, after all, they were plastic. Wherever they were in their real lives, they wouldn't know, and the main thing was for them to be safe from discovery. He laid another plank shelf across the top.

Suddenly he stiffened, raising his head. He thought he heard— He rushed to the narrow window and leaned out, calling. But no. It must have been another cat.

*　　　*　　　*

It took about three weeks to settle in. Omri and Gillon started school in the local comprehensive. They could get there in ten minutes on their bikes through the country lanes. It was a far cry from Gillon's predicted "tinny country school with eight pupils"; it had over a thousand, and felt strange at first. Mrs. Everest (whom Omri called Tea Cozy but the other kids called Peaky) turned out to be all right—strict, but okay. Nobody could get her wig to fall off, and rumor had it it was glued on. Omri's form teacher was a middle-aged man named John Butcher. Obviously he didn't need a nickname.

Adiel set off for boarding school, a big one outside Bristol. He had all his things in a trunk, rather like Omri's old chest only made of metal. They wouldn't see him again till half-term. Omri missed him and didn't miss him. Even when he missed him, he didn't miss him half as much as he missed Kitsa.

He was sure now she would never come back. He tried to resign himself, to think of her being free, enjoying the naturalness of her new life, but the trouble was, she wasn't used to the country and when he let himself think about it, he didn't see how she would manage. She'd never hunted in her life, beyond a halfhearted pounce at the odd bird— and the time she'd nearly killed Boone, of course, but that was just a fluke.

And there was worse. They hadn't been there a week before a fox got into the henhouse and killed three of their hens. If it could do that, it could surely kill a little town cat. Thoughts of her nagged him like an aching tooth he kept biting on to see if it still hurt.

One evening at supper—meals were only just stopping being picnics—Omri's father said, "Oh, by the way, Omri. I was talking to the bank manager today. Your mysterious package has arrived at the local branch and is in the safe."

Gillon looked up. He hadn't heard anything about the package till now. "What's this?" he asked.

"Nothing," said Omri quickly, and signaled his father, who caught on at once and refused to say any more.

Gillon, however, wouldn't leave it alone.

"What package? What was Dad talking about?"

"Oh, mind your own business!" Omri yelled at last.

That was it for the moment, but the next day at school, Gillon found Omri on the playground and said cockily, "I know what your mystery package is."

"You do not."

"I do. It's your cupboard, isn't it?"

Omri felt the blood rush to his head. He gaped at Gillon.

"Your face! Did you think I didn't know?"

"Know . . . what?" Omri half gasped.

"That you're hooked on it. But putting it in the bank? Pretending it's valuable? Get real. The bank's only for really valuable things, like jewelry or gold."

Omri bit his tongue and said nothing. He kicked the turf and stared at the toe of his trainer.

"If I told Dad what it was—"

"Tell him if you like."

"*If* I told him, he'd go straight away and get it out. It's using up space. The bank safe isn't for toys."

"You gave it to me. You should be pleased I l-like it."

"Yeah, but—the *bank*—It's just stupid." They stood for a moment, staring out across the acres of green, so huge, so different from the hemmed-in tarmac playground in town. "There's nothing special about it. Is there?"

"It's special to me. It was smashed up in the storm, and I mended it. I don't want anything else to happen to it."

"And did you put the key with it?"

Now Omri visibly jumped. "What key?"

"The one you locked the cupboard with when you were playing with it. The one with the red ribbon that Mum used to wear on a chain."

Omri felt winded. He couldn't think what to say, and every second he didn't turn it all off with some careless remark made it more obvious to Gillon that he'd stumbled on a really important secret. He was staring at Omri now with an ever more beady look of interest and excitement.

"I know there's more to that cupboard than you're telling," he said at last. "I'm sorry I laughed about the bank. Maybe it really is valuable. I wish you'd tell me."

There was a long silence. Then Omri suddenly shouted, "Well I'm not going to!"

Turning, he ran fast toward the hedge at the far side of the playground. It was about a hundred yards away. When he got there, panting, he sat down on the grass in a hidden place. Gillon hadn't followed him.

Omri put his head on his knees. He was shaking. Something terrible had almost happened. *He had had a strong urge to tell Gillon.* He had wanted to tell him. Gillon of all people, who made fun of him, who could never in a million years keep such a secret to himself. What had come over him? Why had he had to run away fast to stop himself from blurting it out?

He didn't understand this feeling. It felt more like loneliness than anything else. People did really crazy things when they were lonely. But how could he be? He had his family, he was making new friends at school. . . . Of course he missed Patrick . . . and Emma . . . and what he thought about as "the old world." But that wasn't it.

It couldn't be old Kits, could it? You couldn't miss a cat so badly that it made you weak and apt to do stupid things, blurt out a vital secret just to share it with someone?

He'd have to watch himself.

He heard the bell in the distance. He got up slowly and walked back to the school, saying over and over again, "Never. Never. Never. Never must I tell."

THREE

Hidden in the Thatch

Omri's father lost little time in getting the re-thatching of the roof underway.

He had been making inquiries among neighbors and people in their local village and pretty soon some men arrived in a beat-up old car to inspect and measure the roof and talk money. A very great deal of it. That evening Omri saw his mother carrying a large tumbler of brown liquid across the lane to the big workshop his father had adopted as a painting studio.

"Is that whiskey, Mum?" asked Omri with interest. (The cowboy, Boone, had been a great whiskey drinker, but his father wasn't.)

"Yes," said his mother somewhat grimly. "Your

father has had a shock. Alcohol was invented for times like this."

"How much of a shock?"

"Fifteen thousand pounds' worth," she replied.

"Blimey! Just for a bit of straw?"

"Just for a bit of straw."

But it wasn't only for that, of course, his mother explained. Thatching was a skilled craft, and not many people still knew how to do it properly. And it wasn't straw. It was reeds, and the right sort only came from a particular place in France, because in Britain the reed beds were protected and couldn't be used. The work would take about four weeks. And they had to do it at once because it couldn't be done in winter—the whole of the roof had to come off.

"Like when the storm blew our other roof off!" said Omri the next day at tea when all this was being gone into.

"Dad, its going to be so cold!" said Gillon.

But their father said tersely, "We'll all have to be *terribly* brave about that, won't we, Gillon?"

"Lucky old Ad, safe and snug at school," muttered Gillon, who certainly hadn't shown any envy for his older brother so far.

"Look out of the window, boys," said their mother suddenly. "We've got visitors."

They went to the window. On the lawn were three large magpies, gleaming black and white in

the sun, strutting about and pecking at something
that lay in the long grass.

Omri had a moment of absolute horror. He knew
magpies were scavenger birds—he'd seen them
pecking at the remains of one of the fox-killed hens.
What could be lying there, dead?

He rushed out of the house, his heart in his
throat. The birds flapped unconcernedly away just
as he reached them. Hardly able to bear his appre-
hension, Omri parted the grass and looked at the
corpse.

It was a half-grown rabbit without a head.

The others, belatedly realizing what Omri had
feared, trailed out after him.

"It's not her, is it?" called his mother.

"It's a dead rabbit," said Omri.

"Yuck," said Gillon. "Those magpies have eaten
half of it."

Their father bent down to look at it more closely.

"I don't think the magpies killed it," he said.
"Too big for them. It would take a fox to kill that,
and why would he have left it half eaten? Looks
more like a cat's work to me."

Omri gazed at the dead half-rabbit with entirely
new eyes.

"You mean—a cat could kill a thing that size?
You mean maybe Kitsa could have hunted it?"

"It's possible," he said.

Omri's heart did an upward lurch. The hope he

had abandoned rushed back, painfully, like the blood coming back into a numbed limb.

"But if she's around, why doesn't she come home?"

"Maybe she's gone feral," said his father.

"Gone feral? What's that?"

"Wild. Cats do. Mainly tomcats, but queens do as well sometimes, when they're moved. I bet she's around, Omri. Keep your eyes open for her, and keep putting out her milk."

Omri put not milk but clotted cream out for her that night. In the morning it was gone.

"Probably a hedgehog," said Gillon.

Omri wanted to hit him, but he felt too relieved. There *was* hope, after all.

The thatchers arrived to begin work, and chaos came again to the just-organized-after-moving household.

The garden, the hedge, the border of the lane, and all the paths vanished under masses of moldy old thatch as the thatching team tore it off the roof beams. There was no point in clearing most of it till the job was done, but Omri was told to keep the route from the lane gate to the front of the house cleared. He did this after school. Every day for the first week it had to be done again. It was absolutely amazing how much old thatch there was—enough to make three or four haystacks. It kept piling up all around the house.

The thatchers expected regular cups of tea, and when the weather turned really hot at the end of September, relays of beer. They got chatty. In breaks, they sat out on the thatch-littered lawn and discussed their craft with anyone in the family who would join them.

One afternoon after school, Omri was drifting past and heard one of them say, "We ent found that oul' bottle yet. Last chaps hid it thorough, seemingly."

He paused. "What old bottle?"

The men grinned. "Don' ee know about the thatchers' bottle?"

"No?"

"We were tellin' your dad. Right int'rested, he be. Wants to see un when we find un."

"But what is it?"

"It's like this here, see. Every time a roof gets thatched, which is about every thirty year, the thatchers all writes their names on a paper—"

"On'y in the olden days they'm put a cross instead—"

"And any details as is relevant to the job, and puts it in a bottle, along with the papers from the thatchers as done the last job, and the one afore that. And they hides it in the thatch, for the next ones to find, thirty year on."

"That way," put in another, "there's a link, see,

from one generation of thatchers to the next, down the line, maybe 'undreds o' years. This 'ouse now, it's been standin' not far short o' three 'undred year, wouldn't ee say, John?''

"Since 1704," said Omri eagerly. "The plaque says."

"Arh, the plaque, well there you are then. Musta bin—let's see—between seven and nine thatchin's in that time, maybe more, so it'll be a ruddy big oul' bottle I reckon, when we do find un." They all laughed and swigged their lager.

Omri was intrigued about the bottle, and so was his father.

"A real link with the past," he kept saying. "If they find it, I'm going to make photocopies of all the papers, to keep, before they add their one and hide the bottle again."

"Can we keep the old bottle, Dad?"

"No. They use the same one till it gets broken. That's the custom. I love old country customs. I respect them. A real link with the past!"

"Yeah, Dad, you said that," said Gillon, who found the whole thing a total turnoff.

That night Omri lay awake in his new room, under the denuded roof and bare eaves, with the window open.

The milk dish had been empty again this morning, and he'd wanted to keep watch all night, but of course his mother wouldn't let him. It was hard to fall asleep anyway. He was so used to traffic going past all night, and London streetlamps lighting the room, he still wasn't quite used to the darkness and quiet of the country.

Not that it was dark tonight. There was a full moon. It bathed the surrounding hills, fields, and woods, and shone down through a little tear in the roofers' tarpaulin over his head. It was a bit like his old room where he'd slept on a platform under a skylight. It had felt like sleeping out under the sky.

Suddenly he sat up. He'd heard a cry. It sounded just like the cry of a cat in distress!

Without thinking he jumped up and rushed through Gillon's room (that he had to pass through to get to the stairs) and fumbled his way down and out into the soft-scented, unfamiliar, mildly scary country night, full of rustlings and creature noises that you never heard in London.

In bare feet and by the clear light of the moon, he kicked through the fallen thatch, crossed the sloping lawn, let himself out through a little picket gate, and started pushing through the overgrown grass in the paddock, calling softly, "Kitsa! Kitsa, come on, Kits!" and making shwsh-a-wisha noises that used to bring her running. His feet were stung with stinging nettles and pricked with thistles, but

he kept going until he stepped in an old cowpat—
that was too much!

"Bloody *country*!" he exploded, and turned back,
but not before he'd had a long listen. He couldn't
hear her now. It must have been a bird or something. He scraped his foot on the damp grass to
clean it. Then he picked his way back toward the
front door.

It occurred to him just as he was about to go in,
to have a look to see if the milk had been drunk
yet. Instead of walking in the front door and out
again at the back, because of his mucky foot he
decided to walk around the outside to the kitchen
door, which he did, treading on layers of old thatch
all the way. And while he was passing under the
plaque on the gable end, he nearly twisted his ankle
stepping on something lumpy and hard.

It didn't feel like a stone, so he fumbled about
in the thatch to see what it was—maybe it was "the
oul' bottle"! It would be fun if he could be the one
to find it, not the thatchers at all!

The rotted reeds had all matted together and
must have fallen off the roof in a clump, instead
of in thousands of loose bits like most of it. It
felt disgusting to his groping fingers, and the smell
of mustiness and rot—which pervaded the whole
house—was very strong. Yet in the middle of it
was undoubtedly something solid.

He fished it out. It wasn't a bottle, old or otherwise. It was an oblong package wrapped in blackened, disintegrating cloth and tied with thick string that came apart at his first tentative tug.

He dropped the string on the path and moved back to the front of the house, into full moonlight. The bit of cloth was thick and heavy, like canvas. Omri carefully unwrapped it. His heart was beating very hard for some reason. He was suddenly terribly excited. What could this possibly be, that someone had hidden in the thatch perhaps as much as thirty years ago?

Inside the wrapping was a small black metal cashbox with a curved brass handle. It had a slot in the top to put coins in, but this was sealed with some lumpy hard stuff. It was very firmly locked. Separate from it was another, flat package that had lain under the box inside the cloth.

When Omri unfolded this second piece of canvas, he found a thick notebook inside. It had a leather cover with metal corners, and it was full of writing.

Unluckily, Gillon woke up as Omri was creeping through his room to get back to his own, and got a fright.

"Who's there! Who's there!" he yelled right out loud. The next minute their father had come crashing through Omri's room from the parents' room beyond that.

He switched on the light and Omri stood revealed. He thrust his find up his pajama jacket and in the sudden blaze of light on everyone's sleepy eyes, nobody saw him do it.

"Omri! What do you think you're doing at this hour!"

"I—I thought I heard Kitsa crying."

"Blasted cat! She's all right! Go to bed."

"I'm just going. Sorry. Sorry, Gillon."

Gillon, still half asleep, mumbled something and rolled over. The light went out and Omri followed his father into his own room. His father then went through the other side into his bedroom. Omri shut both doors. Privacy—there wasn't any. He was going to have to do something about this.

Trembling with excitement, he lay down on the bed and waited till everything was quiet. The pattern of moonlight had altered as the moon began to set. He got up and sat in its beam and set the cashbox on the floor. He opened the notebook.

On the first page were a few words in the most beautiful delicate handwriting. He could just about read them, although the ink had faded to a pale brown.

Account of My Life, and of a Wonder Unacceptable to the Rational Mind. To be hidden until a time when Minds in my Family may be more Open.

There was a name. A three-word name. In the wan light of the setting moon Omri could hardly read it till he carried the notebook to the window.

The name was Jessica Charlotte Driscoll. And there was a date. August 21, 1950.

August the twenty-first! Another sign—another coincidence, like the LB on the plaque! August 21 was Omri's birthday.

Jessica Charlotte Driscoll.

The name Driscoll meant nothing to Omri. Nor did Jessica. But Charlotte! Charlotte was the name that Lottie was short for. And Lottie had been Omri's mother's mother's name.

But the moment the thought crossed his mind that this could be *that* Charlotte—his grandmother—he banished it instantly. That was impossible. His grandmother had died in the bombing of London in World War Two, when his own mother was only a few months old. By 1950 she would have been dead for eight years.

Anyway, even though this house had been owned by some distant cousin, any connection between it and his grandmother was impossible. She had lived in south London all her short life. His mother had told Omri that the only place his grandmother'd ever visited out of London was Frinton, a seaside place where her sailor husband had taken her on their honeymoon.

No, all right. So this Charlotte wasn't a relative.

Or was she? She must have been living here
before the elderly cousin who had recently died. If
she'd been a relative of his, she might also be a
relative of Omri's.

Omri dared not switch the light on and start to
read the notebook because there weren't curtains
yet, and his parents would be sure to see the light
through their window. He had to compose his soul
in patience till morning. He slept uneasily with the
notebook under his pillow, and the cashbox—the
cashbox! what could be in there?—hidden under
the bed.

A Wonder Unacceptable to the Rational
Mind. . . .

Omri knew a bit about that. "There's real magic
in this world. . . ." Even Patrick knew it now.
Patrick the practical, the doubter, the one who'd
once tried to pretend none of it had happened.
They'd had proof enough to convince anyone. A
little bathroom cabinet that, when you locked it
with a special key, became a magic box that brought
plastic toy figures to life. And more than that—
they were not just "living dolls," but real people,
magicked from their lives in the past.

Little Bear had been the first, and, for Omri,
would always be the most special—an Iroquois Indian from the late eighteenth century, coming from
a village in what was now the state of New York.
Then had come others: Tommy, the soldier-medic,

who'd later been killed; Boone, the cowboy (he was really Patrick's special pal), and Bright Stars, Little Bear's wife, and her baby who had been born while she was with them. Matron, the strict but staunch nurse from a London hospital of the 1940's. And Corporal—now Sergeant—Fickits, the Royal Marine who had helped them defeat the skinhead gang that had broken into Omri's old house. . . .

They were so real! So much a part of Omri's life . . . It was hard to keep his vow to do without them, to eschew the magic. But he must. Because it could be dangerous. The storm that had wrecked half of England had been brought by them, with the key. People had been killed . . . in the present, and in the past. It was frightening. It was too much to handle.

And now—*A Wonder Unacceptable to the Rational Mind* . . .

Omri gave a little shiver, half fear, half excitement, and slept. He dreamed of riding with Little Bear through the hills and forests of his homeland. Awake and asleep he often dreamed of him, but this was particularly vivid and the ride was magical and wonderful. It seemed as if Little Bear were teaching him to ride, and at the same time, as if they were searching for something. Some treasure.

He meant to wake up early—at dawn—and read the notebook, but of course he slept in. There was no time, none at all. He hid the notebook behind some books and went down to breakfast.

At the table he asked, as casually as he could, "Mum, what relative of ours exactly was the old man who owned this house?"

"Ah! Now you're asking . . ." She paused with the cereal package poised, her brow wrinkling. "Let me see. Well, his name was Frederick, which is a bit of a family name on my side. He was a bachelor. And very old indeed—about eighty-five. I *think* he was—wait for it—my grandmother's younger sister's son. Yes, that's it, I remember now. I never knew him or had any connection with him."

"What was his last name?" asked Omri, frowning.

"An Irish name—it's slipped my mind for the moment."

"How come you didn't know him if he was your cousin?"

"Well, that's a story. My grandmother, who brought me up after Mummy died, didn't see her sister for some reason, though when I was little she talked about her sometimes, in a—a sort of *head shaking* way, as if she loved her a lot but felt she shouldn't. Of course I found that intriguing and asked lots of questions about her, but my granny just said, 'Well, we were sisters, but I have to say it: She was no better than she should be.' "

"What does that mean?"

"She had a Past. You weren't supposed to have

a Past in those days. Something scandalous to do with men. . . .''

Omri digested this. Then he asked slowly, "Could she have been living here—your granny's sister?''

His mother looked at him. "She was supposed to have gone abroad . . . But what an intriguing idea, Omri! I never thought of that. Maybe old Frederick inherited this house from his mother, who was my wicked great-aunt Jessica Charlotte!''

Omri put down his spoon. There was some saying he'd always thought very silly, about a goose walking over your grave. But suddenly he understood it because the bumpy flesh all over his arms had the chill feeling of death.

"Was she really wicked?'' he asked after a moment.

"I've no idea. She was some kind of actress back around the time of the First World War. Going on the stage in those days was considered fairly wicked by some people. But I'm sure there was more to it than that. Now darling, enough questions, it's ten to nine. Go.''

Omri didn't think about Kitsa more than half a dozen times that day. Nor did he give too much attention to lessons, and the Butcher had occasion to send him to the Tea Cozy, who gave him what-for without too much care for his feelings and added injury to insult with a detention. *Murphy's law in*

action, he thought furiously. *If anything can go wrong, it will, and at the worst possible time.* He was absolutely dying to get home.

By the time the Butcher let him go and he had raced home through the lanes on his bike (narrowly avoiding being run down by a tractor—well, better than a London bus!) he couldn't possibly be bothered to clear the last of the thatch from the path properly. He just kicked it aside as he forged up the path and raced to his room.

He shut both doors and put some spare bricks against them so they wouldn't open easily. Then he extracted the thick notebook from behind his books and opened it with hands that were not quite steady.

He read the words on the flyleaf again.

Account of My Life, and of a Wonder Unacceptable to the Rational Mind. To be hidden until a time when Minds in my Family may be more Open.

Jessica Charlotte Driscoll.
AUGUST 21, 1950.

He turned the page and began to read the fine, beautifully formed handwriting.

FOUR

Jessica Charlotte's Notebook

I write this on my deathbed.

Since I have not seen or heard anything from Maria for nearly half a lifetime, I cannot be sure she has not gone before me—though I have my own reason for believing she will out-live me by many years. . . . Still, sooner or later we must come face to face on the Other Side. Much as I have missed and longed for her, I am in no great hurry to meet her there. Strange but true: I fear God in His Almighty Power less than I fear facing my sister Maria.

I am still at heart an *artiste*. So I write this account as a kind of rehearsal of what I shall say to her—and Him. I shall excuse nothing, omit nothing, extenuate nothing. When I look now into the glass on the front of the wondrous Cabinet Frederick made with such anger in his heart (which sits on the table by my bedside), I see, not my face, but Death's. It tells me sternly that "naught now availeth" but scrupulous Truth.

My Little People would speak for me, if they could. They've seen the best in me. With them, at least, I've dealt honestly and kindly. I have not shown them my accursed jealousy and spite.

But they must Go Back, pursue their own lives and make their own accounting at last. Though I still bring them sometimes, when I'm lonely and afraid, to comfort and distract me, they can't help me now. Even though Jenny weeps (tears that are as small as points of starlight) when I tell her I'm dying. She weeps for herself, also. . . . What will become of her? I can't send *her* back now.

I don't deserve the Wonder that has been my consolation at the end of my misspent life.

When Omri reached this point in the notebook, he found his heart was beating so hard and his breath had been caught in his lungs without breathing out for so long that he had to stop.

He swallowed, shut his eyes so he couldn't read

the delicate brown writing, and breathed in and out several times until his heartbeats slowed. He felt dizzy, confused. There was a faint sheen of sweat on his face. The "wondrous Cabinet" in which she could see her face in a "glass"! The Little People from another time! Was this real? Was he really reading about IT—*his own cupboard? Was it conceivable that this great-great aunt of his had had it in this very house, over thirty years ago?*

To rehearse my story, I must tell it all, from the beginning. And then I must do what I must do, and Maria will know my guilty secret.

Maria, my beautiful elder sister . . . Everything came to her, without her even trying. Our parents' favor. The admiration of friends and relations. The chances in life that make all the difference. And the love of a man. In that too, she was luckier than me. *Her* love was honest and true.

I hated her at times.

There, it's out. My jealous spirit infected me like a virus. I wanted to *be her*, and I was not, so I hated her for her beauty, and for the way she attracted love. And for being good.

Everyone praised her goodness. Was it all true? Was she really, deeply, *better* than I? Had she been me—little, plump, plain, mocked, ignored, where she was tall and graceful and clever—would she have been so moral then?

Who can tell.

When she was barely sixteen, her suitors were already crowding our house. I remember them, callow young men, bringing her presents, fawning on her, while I silently watched. . . . But I didn't stay silent! Oh, no!

After they'd gone, I would mimic them. Mercilessly! I would *force* Maria to laugh at their antics even when she had thought she admired them.

"Oh, stop, Jessie, stop!" she'd cry, weeping with laughter. "You are a demon, you've caught him *exactly* with his funny walk and his lisp. Oh, stop it, I will never be able to look at him again!"

She was my first audience. Those were my moments of fulfillment when I forgot my plainness and began to be an actress.

But there was something else about me, and this I kept to myself. *I knew things.* I knew she was not going to marry any of these. I knew what would be. Oh, not everything! But certain flashes of future knowledge came to me, even as a child.

I had a dream, I had it over and over again, of myself standing in a building that was half lit and half dark. I stood high, and many people faced me from below, and I could do as I pleased with them—make them laugh or cry or sing or cheer, at my will. It was a theater, of course, but I didn't know it then—how could I? I had never seen one. My father thought a theater was the devil's own den.

But as I grew up, I learned about the world. Actors were not "respectable" but they were much talked of . . . and I found out the meaning of my dream, and I knew my destiny.

When I told our father I was going on the stage for a living, he told me—and meant it—that he would rather see me dead in my coffin. He refused to consider it. I was punished for dreaming of it.

To actually do it meant leaving home, enduring disgrace, being cast out, abandoning all that was familiar and safe . . . It meant being poor, living alone, begging for jobs, mixing with every sort of person. Yet I did it. I am still proud of that. It took a lot of courage. Somehow I achieved my ambition, and my father—though he never forgave me—at least noticed me and came to know that I was not the little nobody-and-nothing he had always thought me.

And Maria stood by me. Not openly, of course, but secretly.

It was the first time she had ever deceived

our parents or gone against her "good" character. But she loved me and she visited me. No one knew. But it counted.

When my chance came and I did my first "turn" on the stage of the Hackney Empire music hall, she was there in the stalls. What courage! We both had to be brave that night. I remember her, sitting alone—well, unescorted, at a time when women didn't go anywhere without a man—in her big hat and her pretty furs, laughing aloud as she used to laugh in our bedroom when I mocked her suitors, and she gave me confidence, more than the rest of the laughter.

Because I knew that if I were not truly funny, she would not have laughed. She was my sister, but she wouldn't pretend—she wanted me to give up and come home and be her poor little second-rate sister again. She wanted my talent to be for her alone.

A debt was owed for those acts of loyalty and courage. How did you repay her, Jessica Charlotte?

And that wasn't all. When my Frederick was going to be born, I had to go away to hide my shame, and I couldn't work, and was destitute.

It was then I came to this house for the first time. It was still a farmhouse then and the farmer's wife was a relative of my young man.

I will not name him . . . I have forgotten him! He wasn't worthy to be remembered! But he made her take me in (it was the last thing he ever did for me) and Frederick was born here, here in this very room in this old house in the Hidden Valley—how rightly named! I was hiding at last, ashamed at last, I who had stood brazenly on a stage for men to look at, and sworn that I would never be ashamed. I was ashamed of my child, of my own son.

Perhaps Fred felt it, even then, and that was why he never loved or forgave me.

Maria, though she couldn't come so far from home without arousing our parents' suspicion, wrote to me secretly and sent me money. She understood by now about love, for she was in love with Matthew Darren. I was to meet him in time, and she would say, her face all a blaze of love: "Well? Can you mock him, can you turn me off him?" and I had to say "No." He was above my mockery and my mimicry. . . .

I never saw a woman so fond as she was of him. But there was a long delay before they could be married because he was working in India, and our father would not allow her to go out there to that tropical climate that he said would kill her. The Old Queen was dead and her son fat Edward too, before they were wed at last, and a year later Lottie was born.

Little Lottie. My sweet, adorable niece. My little girl whom I wronged. There can be no forgiveness!

I am crying. . . . Let me rest. I can write no more for the present.

FIVE

Family Stuff

"Gilly."

"Oh, *what?*"

"Sorry to interrupt. What are you doing, anyway?"

"Homework," said Gillon virtuously.

"You're not—are you really?"

"If I don't I'm seriously stitched up. It's last week's. Pit Bull'll tear me to pieces."

"Ah." Mr. Pitt was indeed fiercer than Mr. Butcher.

"What did you want?" asked Gillon.

"Just to ask you something. You know the cupboard."

"The precious cupboard, taking up space in the bank safe! Yeah?"

"Where did you get it?"

Gillon was silent for a long moment. Too long. Then he said, "I told you at the time. Found it in the alley behind our old house. Our old-old house, the one before last."

"No, you didn't."

Gillon sat at his desk without turning, but there was something about the back of his neck that told Omri he was right.

"How do you know?"

"I just do. Tell me where you got it really."

Gillon turned on his swivel chair. "Listen"—he began. Then he stopped, frowned, and said, "What's up with you? You look funny."

"Funny how?"

"I dunno, as if you were zonked out. Look, so what if I made it up about the alley? I didn't pretend I'd paid for it. I said I'd found it, and that was true. I thought the alley would make it more sort of— interesting."

"Go on."

"Well. I found it in our basement. Among a whole lot of stuff. Most of it was just junk. Ask me, that cupboard was junk too, only you were gone on secret drawers and boxes and stuff and I thought you might think it was a bit of fun. I was skint at the time, it was the best I could do for a birthday present for you. I didn't expect you to go crazy over it."

"Whose was it?"

"Mum's, I suppose. All the junk that collects in our houses is hers."

"And did you ask her—you know, if you could have it to give me?"

"Well, no. I didn't think she'd miss it. And she never recognized it, did she? She never knew she had it."

This was evidently true. His mother hadn't flickered an eyelid when Omri had unwrapped Gillon's present. It was because she had such a lot of stuff, half of it just bunged down in the cellar (or, in the next house, in the attic) without much sorting. His mother just couldn't throw anything away—when they'd moved here, to this much smaller house with no attics or cellars, she'd stored all her "family stuff," as she called it, in the outbuilding that had once been a pigsty.

Family stuff . . .

He went to look for his mother, and found her feeding the hens. She looked so countrified, scattering the corn with great sweeps of her arm like the sower-of-seed in the picture, Omri would have laughed if he hadn't been feeling so solemn.

"Mum."

"Yes, darling."

"You know all your family stuff."

"Oh, don't talk about it! I *really must* sort it out one of these days." She'd been saying that at intervals for as long as Omri could remember.

"Where did it come from?"

"My grandmother mostly."

"Her name was Maria, wasn't it?"

"Yes. Granny Marie I used to call her."

"When did she die?"

"Oh, not till I was grown-up. Adiel was a baby. I have a photo somewhere of her, holding him in her arms. She was really old—well into her eighties."

So Maria was not waiting for her sister on the Other Side. Jessica Charlotte herself would have had a long wait—nearly twenty years—for the chance to explain. Explain what?

Omri had had to stop reading the notebook for the moment. He felt too wound up. The story was too—too strong for him to take in much at a time. That poor old lady, dying all alone like that, feeling so bad. . . . Now, getting himself ready to read on, he was doing some investigating.

"What about your grandfather?"

"Matt. Poor Matt. Well, I never knew him. He died long before my time, when my mother was only a child."

"Lottie . . ."

"Yes."

"Did he die—abroad?"

His mother looked at him curiously. "No. He spent years in the colonies as an administrator, but—no. He died in London, in an accident. Terribly sad. Granny Marie never got over it. Just think of losing your husband, and then your only daughter in the bombing . . ."

"She had you."

"Yes. And I loved her. But we were very hard up—Matt's pension was pitifully small. We rented a little house in the East End, and Granny Marie had to work until she was quite old—it was a hard life for her, but she never let me feel it. I had a very happy childhood, thanks to her."

Omri went back upstairs. Gillon met him at the top.

"Don't you want to watch TV? Rats to homework, there's a great film on."

"No, thanks," said Omri. "I'm busy."

He piled the bricks against his doors again and went to the window. The sun was sinking behind the hills in front of the house. There was one special hill with a little crown of trees that grew in a cluster, in odd shapes—all spready and twisted. Omri wanted to go up there one day to see what they were like close to. With school and everything, and the thatching, there hadn't been much time to explore.

Now when he looked at the view he thought of

Jessica Charlotte, looking at the same one. Which had been her bedroom? Not this one. Gillon's. He felt sure of it. He'd found the box and the notebook at the gable end of the house. She must have hidden it in the eaves outside her window—the last window of the longhouse.

He unearthed the cashbox from its hiding place and looked at it again. The coin slot was bunged up with some hard red stuff. Omri thought it might be sealing wax, he'd seen it on documents in museums. Ordinary people used to seal their letters with it in the old days. . . . Why would she seal it? To keep the damp out, of course.

He shook the box gently, trying to guess what was in it. There were a number of things in there, but they seemed to be wrapped because they slid about whisperingly; they didn't rattle. Of course he could break it open . . . But he didn't want to. She'd sealed and locked and hidden it, for him— for someone *in the family with a mind more open*—to find in years to come. When he had read the rest of the notebook, he would know whether she wanted him to open it and how it could be done.

He put the box away again, and with a strange, solemn feeling of destiny—yes, destiny, this was *meant* to happen—he pulled his desk chair close to the window and opened the notebook at the place where he had left off.

After Frederick was born, I *had* to work. It was not merely to fulfill my ambition and my talent then. I had a hungry baby with no father to feed him—so I had to do whatever came to hand.

I won't recount everything I did in those years to earn money. On the stage, off the stage . . . It was a strange life. One week I would be topping the bill at some provincial music hall, the crowd at my feet, the stage-door johnnies bringing me flowers and sweets and trinkets and making much of me. The next I might be behind a bar in some city pub, joking with the customers and pretending to drink the drinks they bought me but secretly pocketing their money and wetting my lips with the cold tea I kept under the bar.

Once I scrubbed steps . . . No matter. Let the past bury its dead. Frederick, who spent his babyhood in a Moses basket under many theatrical dressing tables, grew up to hate the business . . . but he grew straight and strong and with a will of iron. I thought I had cause to be satisfied with him, at least. Little did I know what a strange man my child would grow into.

And Maria?

My lucky, spoiled sister married her Matthew at last and had Lottie. Charlotte she was christened, not after me, of course—the family black sheep—but after our grandmother. But I was there! I crept into the church at Maria's secret bidding, in my sober Sunday clothes with a big brimmed hat pulled well down so no one would know me. Father and Mother were both dead by then, and our other relatives hadn't seen me for ten hard, aging years. . . . I hid behind a pillar and pretended I was holding the baby, that she was my godchild. . . . A godmother! Me! What nonsense. But all the best parts of my life have been make-believe.

And I looked at Matthew. Maria's Matthew.

Matthew stood by the font, tall as a soldier. Handsome, and generous, and good. I could have loved him myself—I did love him, not least because he didn't cast me out. Of course he never acknowledged me publicly, but he never forbad me to come to their house to visit Maria and Lottie. When no one else was there.

Of course I never brought Frederick. That would never have done! Maria never knew Frederick. Never asked about him. She played the game called "It-Never-Happened."

Those were happy days. I played with my little niece and came to love her then. Beautiful, sweetest Lottie, my namesake, my darling.

But my life was hard. I never told Maria how hard, and of course she never visited me in my sordid lodgings. . . . She was so happy, she didn't want to know anything unpleasant about my life and I never told her. But as I watched her, growing more beautiful and more beloved in wifehood and motherhood, the old bitterness raised its head again. Once more, all I had were crumbs from her table. Crumbs of happiness spilled from her overflowing life.

And one day as I sat in her elegant parlor, playing with Lottie who was then about five, Maria said, very casually but as if she had been preparing it for a long time, "Of course, Jessie, when Lottie is a bit more grown-up, it won't do for you to see so much of her. Matt's a good Christian but there is a limit to tolerance."

I felt her words like a knife. I would be a bad influence! That's what she was saying! That I would contaminate Lottie's life!

I put Lottie, who had been on my knee, down very carefully and stood up. My sister must have seen in my eyes how deeply wounded I was, for she said quickly, "Come along now, darling, don't take me up like that! I don't mean *now*. I just wanted to—to get you used to the idea that one day—"

I should have followed my impulse, and left then, and never come back. But I couldn't.

Frederick was already showing signs of the hostility to me that would pain me so much when he was a man, and I needed this other home, I needed Maria and her crumbs of love. I needed Lottie. I needed the glimpses I got of Matthew. . . . Crumbs indeed. But I was so hungry!

Yet the iron entered my soul. A deep bitterness about the differences between us. My idea—my terrible, wicked idea—came to me soon afterward, when the shadow of her words about Lottie was still darkening my heart.

No excuses, I said. No excuses! Tell the tale.

We were in Maria's boudoir. (Yes! She had one—a room all to herself, for her to dress in and do her hair and entertain her friends, and be herself, a room of feminine fancies and personal things, where even Matthew did not come without a knock!) And she was showing me her jewelry.

It was kept in a special jewel case—a piece of barefaced luxury that Matthew had bought her on their wedding trip to Florence, in Italy. It was red leather tooled in gold, lined with red satin, with little trays that lifted apart on delicate hinges. And at every level were the tokens of Matthew's love for her, and our mother's, for Mama had left all her pretty things to Maria. I in my disgrace had been left nothing.

There was plenty there that I would have liked: a pearl necklace, two gold lockets, an emerald bracelet, even a fine diamond pin— Mama's wedding present from Papa that she had once said should come to me. But then, in the bottom, I saw them. A pair of earrings.

Beautiful! Oh, yes, they were. But more than that. They held my eyes like buttons in buttonholes.

They were aquamarines, like two tear-shaped drops of seawater. Not our gray sea, no, but like the seas of the south that I had seen paintings of, blue-green, clear, without a flaw. They hung from two gold hooks.

And I wanted them. I wanted them! To me they suddenly stood for all Maria had, and that I had not, all she wanted to shut me out from when my Lottie would be older. Not least her purity—my sister was pure as a perfect jewel.

I made up my mind in that single instant that those earrings would be mine. And I knew clearly that there was only one way that could happen. I would steal them.

That night when his mother came to kiss him in bed, as she always did, Omri pulled her to sit down beside him.

"Mum, why was your grandmother so poor?"

"As I told you—my grandfather's pension—"

"Yeah, but—you told me ages ago that your grandmother had a jewel case. You know the key— you said it belonged to a jewel case she'd got from Italy."

"Yes, that's right. A red leather one."

"Well, I mean—a jewel case usually has some jewels in it."

"Oh, I see what you mean! Well, it was stolen."

"Stolen!"

"Yes. There was a burglary. Oh, long before I was born—sometime after Matt died. They used to have a lot of lovely things. She told me about her silver tea service and other things they'd had, wedding presents, things her parents left her. . . . It was all stolen. And there was no insurance. She'd stopped paying the premiums after Matthew died. So she lost all her valuables. She had to sell the Clapham Common house and buy a little slummy one. And get a job. Which was no joke for a woman who'd never worked."

"What job?"

"Secretarial. Secretaries were actually called 'typewriters' in those days. My darling old gran was among the legion of post-World-War-One typewriters. She went on doing it till my mother and father were able to help her. Then after they died, she went out cleaning to keep me. She was well into her sixties then."

"Cleaning!" Omri exclaimed. "Do you mean she, like, scrubbed steps?"

His mother closed her eyes for a moment. "I don't know. She might have done. She never talked about it. I hope not. It would have been—such an awful comedown for someone who'd been brought up as she had." She opened her eyes again and looked at him curiously. "You are a funny one," she said. "You've never shown an interest in family history before."

As soon as his mother left, Omri, with new pictures in his head, went back to the Account.

SIX

Pouring the Lead

I did not commit my crime at once.

If I had, perhaps I could be forgiven for it, but for two years it remained undone—long enough to have come to my senses, for my better self to take command. But those beautiful sea-green drops dangled in my future, two demons in disguise—beckoning. I knew I would do it.

At that time Frederick was away at school. Then, as now, that cost money, but I was set heart and soul on his having an education. I had to work harder than ever.

The First World War was a curse to mankind, but a blessing to me. There was war work to be done, and troops to be entertained, and between the one and the other—I spent my days in a sweatshop sewing uniforms, my nights singing, dancing, and acting on stages up and down the land—I scraped by. Even so, I could not have managed, had it not been for my Gift.

I learned the skill of telling fortunes.

Telling fortunes is, in the main, a game of deceit. For ninety-nine out of one hundred in the profession, there is no reading the past or foreseeing the future. They go through an act that is as much make-believe as anything I did on the stage. They give customers what they want: "You will meet a dark stranger. . . . You will have children. . . . You will pass through difficult times to happiness at last. . . ." Falsehood and fakery! And I did my share of that—tea leaves, tarot cards, crystal ball, all the rest of it.

But when I tried pouring lead, a common enough method of fortune-telling at that time, I found that through the lead I could raise my craft to the level of true Art.

Lead-pouring worked like this.

In an old iron saucepan I heated up small pieces of lead, bought cheap from a scrap-metal man. Lead melts at a low temperature, and when all the lumps had dissolved into a liquid

silver mass, I would ask my customer to pour small amounts into a metal bowl of cold water.

With a hiss and a cloud of steam, the lead would solidify again into a random form in the bottom of the bowl. I would get this out and examine it, and in the shape (which was often very strange, resembling, just as clouds can, all manner of animals and objects) I would perceive Portents of the future. True ones.

Once a young woman poured the lead, and instead of fusing together, it all scattered into little bits. In this I read a dangerous carelessness in her nature, and I warned her, and we tried again, and this time there was a death's head. I saw death and nothing else, and though I invented something to please her, I knew as she walked from my dark little basement room up into the sunlit street that she had no time left. Three days later a neighbor told me she had died in an accident in the factory where she worked.

Thus, and through many other proofs, I knew that I had the Gift, and must use it carefully. I became well-known in the profession and many people consulted me, and paid me well. I was able to pay Fred's school fees and put money by. Money I later used to buy this old house where Fred had been born.

I never, never tried to read the fortunes of

those few I loved. Maria, who knew that I earned extra money this way, begged me to tell her fortune, but I never would, let alone Matthew's or Lottie's, or Frederick's, or mine.

But sometimes flashes of insight would come to me, unbidden. I once saw a dark shadow pass over the face of Matthew as he sat in his garden, laughing with Lottie. I fell into a fainting fit, something unheard of for me who (until my recent illness) never had a sick day in my life. . . . Once I saw a diminishing line of Marias going off into the far distance, like the reflection in double mirrors, which might indicate a long life or many descendants.

When these flashes came, I learned to "switch off" something in my head, as we switch off electric lights. *I did not want to know*. When I looked at Lottie (whom, in truth, I loved better than my own child), it was as if I kept my hand on the switch, holding it firmly at the "off" position. I could not have borne to see any bad thing in the future of that child.

Oh, if I had let myself know! But can we change what we are destined for?

Enough repining for what is too late to mend, Jessica Charlotte. *Tell the tale*. The doctor says you haven't much time. . . . The men have come to mend the thatch, so that, however

else I have failed him, I may pass this house
on to Frederick in good condition.

I have thought of my hiding place.

"Omri! OM-RI!"

Omri seemed to wake up. The shouting must
have been going on for some time. He jumped up,
almost dropping the notebook, and rushed to the
door linking his room with Gillon's, which was half
pushed open against the blockage of bricks.

"What, Mum, what's wrong?"

"Are you deaf?" she inquired politely, but she
was obviously annoyed.

"No, Mum."

"Your supper's on the table. I've been calling
and calling. Why have you put those bricks there?
I couldn't get in!"

"That's the idea, Mum. Ever heard of privacy?"

"Don't be cheeky. Privacy doesn't apply to
mothers."

She stalked off. Omri put a marker in the notebook and hid it under his pillow. It was agony to
stop reading—he had never in his whole life, not
even when reading books about Iroquois Indians,
been so caught up in any story.

Wow, he thought, taking deep breaths as if he'd
been swimming underwater, *it's good I've had
some practice keeping secrets. Wish I could tell
someone, though*!

And like an answer to prayer, in the middle of supper the phone rang.

"Omri, it's for you. I think it's Patrick."

Omri jumped up so suddenly, his chair went over backward, and he rushed to the phone, which was in the farthest-along living room.

"Hi, Patrick, is it you?"

"Yeah, listen, I've nagged Mum half to death. She says if you can have me, I can spend half-term with you."

"Hey—brill! When do you get yours? Ours starts next week."

"Ours too. Bit of luck, eh?"

"I've got so much to tell you!" Omri lowered his voice. "I've found something. Something incredible! You won't believe it till you see it so I won't tell you now. By the time you come I'll have fin—I'll know more."

"Is it to do with—?"

"Yes. Oh, this is fantastic! Don't let anything go wrong, promise!"

Back at the table, grinning all over his face, Omri announced Patrick's visit. His parents said fine, why not, Adiel's half-term was different from that of the other two so they couldn't even think of going away. Patrick could keep Omri company.

"What about me?" asked Gillon. "Can I have a mate to stay too?"

Omri's heart sank a bit. Gillon's mates tended

to be rather riotous; their chief recreation was playing very loud pop music and video games. The walls
of this new house were thin. . . . But on the other
hand, it would be good if Gillon were occupied and
not hanging around him and Patrick. So Omri was
grateful when his father said, sure, why didn't Gillon invite one of his old pals.

It was extremely hard for Omri to settle down
to homework or to anything else while the notebook lay under his pillow, calling to him.

His mother had often talked about the way certain books called you when you were really en-
grossed in them and had to put them down. Now
Omri understood. He seemed to be living in Jessica
Charlotte's world.

He could see her in the sweatshop sewing uniforms, with Frederick away at school as Adiel was.
He could see her (with difficulty—he had never
seen a music-hall act) on the stage, singing and
doing imitations and making people laugh. He
could see her sitting in Maria's "boudoir," staring
longingly into the depths of his great-grandmother's jewel case of Florentine leather, the one his
mother had told him about, the one his magic key
had come from. The key that locked the magic cupboard and made plastic toys into real people from
the past.

He was going to learn about this now, how it

had come about. First the key, then the cupboard—
she would come to the cupboard. This notebook
held the whole secret of the magic. It was here in
his hands.

And he was in a hurry. Pressured as he was by the
life around him, he was sorely tempted to just flick
through the thin pages of the notebook, picking out
the bits that concerned him most. Yet he couldn't.

It would have been utterly wrong to do that. He
felt Jessica Charlotte had written this for *him* and
it was necessary to read *all* her words.

Anyway, he was interested in her life—more and
more. He could see beautiful, tall, graceful Maria
in her fine dresses, and handsome Matthew, and
Lottie (his own grandmother), and understood why
Jessica Charlotte dreaded being shut out from that
happy, wealthy world.

Omri already disliked Frederick. All his mother
had been through to bring him up, how could it be
that he didn't love her, that he despised her being
on the stage? Where, come to that, was Frederick
at the time when Jessica Charlotte was writing the
Account—why was she dying here all alone, caring
enough about him to get the house ready to leave
to him, when he couldn't even be bothered to come
and look after her or visit her!

He must have been a right pig, Omri thought.

And where did the cupboard come into it? Omri
couldn't wait to read on, but often he had to wait.

Just as last year, when he had had Little Bear and the others with him and had had to lead a secret life within his everyday one, now it was the same. Life and school went on and he had to act normally. The time he could spare to be alone and read the notebook was strictly limited.

All the time he was reading, he was imagining Jessica Charlotte. Maybe she was wicked—was she really going to steal her sister's earrings?—but he couldn't help liking her and seeing her side. While he read, it was as if he *was* Jessie. As if—almost as much as when he had "gone back" to Little Bear's village, through the magic of the key—he were living in history.

SEVEN

The Day of the Parade

Maria always kept the red jewel case locked. She didn't trust her servants! She hid its little fancy key in a secret drawer in her desk downstairs in the study. She had to press a certain pattern on the inlay, cleverly contrived to spring a catch, and the secret drawer would fly open. . . .

My difficulty was, although I had often seen this happen, from across the room and with my view blocked by Maria's back, I did not know exactly where to press. I doubted if anyone knew, even Matthew.

This was my safeguard. When the earrings were missed, no one would be blamed. Maria

would have to assume she had somehow mis-
laid them herself—she wore them very often
and I had seen her toss them down carelessly
on her dressing table more than once.

I planned with care and cunning, over the
years, how I would copy the key. While Maria's back was turned I would impress it into a
box I had made, in two halves, each full of wax.
This I would take home, and pour plaster into
the mold. I would then smear the plaster "key"
with oil and make another mold with more
plaster, and into this I could pour some of my
liquid lead to have an exact copy.

I carried the little box of wax about with me
in my pocket, waiting, waiting my chance. And
of course it came. Opportunities for mischief
always come.

There came a great day for England, in November 1918. Armistice Day! The Great War
was over. Everyone was rejoicing! And there
was to be a parade, through the streets of London.

The devil that had hold of me made me bold
and reckless. I had a picture in my mind, of
myself like royalty, wearing my theatrical finery—all feathers and furbelows and my bold-
est stage dress, bright red satin trimmed with
black braid—riding my own horse out there
in front of the parade!

Well, I had no horse, but that didn't stop me. I hired one. Yes, I did! I rifled my savings and hired the tallest (and gentlest!) horse the West End Livery Stables had on offer. I told the groom to deck him out in all his brasses, and ribbons in red, white, and blue, and polish his bridle and sidesaddle till they gleamed, and bring him to the starting place. This was to be my moment—my day as it was England's—and I meant to make the most of it!

And then quite suddenly, I thought what would make it all complete. I thought of Lottie!

On the crest of my wave, I took a cab to Maria's. The streets of London were choked with people and traffic—the noise of horns blaring and music and cheering were deafening. But I got through, and crossed the river to Clapham. I beat on her door, and the maid, Millie, let me into the hall. And Matthew came, and Maria. They looked astonished to see me standing there in all my finery.

"I'm going to ride in the parade!" I gasped out. And then I told them what I wanted. *I wanted Lottie to ride with me*—up in front of me on the horse, at the head of the parade!

Maria was horrified. "But it would be dangerous! What if she fell? All those people—she'd be trampled—"

"She won't fall," I said. "I promise you!

Maria, let her do it! It's something she'll never forget—the end of this terrible war—a day of triumph and joy! Don't make her watch it all tamely from a pavement—let her be part of it!"

"But Jessie, she's not even eight years old! What will people think?"

I thought I'd lost. But suddenly to my astonishment, Matthew stepped in.

"Yes!" he said.

I'll never forget it! The way he spoke—what a man! Such a ringing tone of audacious decision!

"Yes, Maria! We'll allow this. The occasion is unique and we must rise to it! Indeed it is something she will remember all her life. And we will go and watch our little daughter on her Victory Ride."

You, reader of the future, mark me. My sister was not defeated yet. She turned to her husband and said, "But in that big crowd, there may be people who will recognize Jessie—people who *know*." And she looked sideways at me, her black-sheep sister.

And Matthew looked at me with fresh eyes, with Maria's eyes, with the eyes of respectable society, and after a long moment he pronounced sentence on me.

"It will not matter just for today, what people see or what they think. Because this is the last time your sister and Lottie will be together."

It was the doom Maria had warned me of, two years before. The time for separating my darling from me forever had come.

I said nothing, but I know I was white to the lips. I stood there in frozen silence and they hurried to fetch Lottie and get her ready. She appeared all in a rush, wearing a fine little riding habit (she was already taking lessons so that she could ride out on Rotten Row in Hyde Park) and clutching a miniature riding crop in her gloved hand, her bowler hat perched on her pretty head, her face flushed with excitement.

"Is it true, Aunt Jessie? Are you really going to let me ride with you in the parade?"

I crouched before her.

"Yes, darling. There is no one in the world I would rather celebrate victory with than you." But my heart and my pure love for her were muddled with fury because Matthew and Maria had blighted my moment of happiness and triumph by casting over it the shadow of separation forever.

It was just after that that my chance came.

Maria called me upstairs to the boudoir, where she was dressing to go to the parade, to give me last minute warnings about taking care of Lottie. And there was the key, by itself on the dressing table, and just for a moment I had the room to myself while Maria went into the bedroom, still calling instructions. In a trice I had whisked out the wax box, opened it, pressed the key firmly into it twice—once for each side—and had it back in its place before she returned.

The cab was waiting for me. Lottie and I got in, leaving her parents to make their way to their viewing point. We drove to the starting place of the parade and found my groom and my horse at the appointed place among all that milling flag-waving crowd. Little Lottie clung to my hand and hopped up and down with excitement, and when she was lifted up before me on the horse, she suddenly turned and threw her arms around my neck.

"Oh, Aunt Jessie, I love you! I love you so much!" she whispered through all the hubbub.

My brain made a phonograph record of those words and I play them when I need them. Never once did Frederick say them to me.

What a ride we had! High up above the crowd with our fine mount clopping along in stately splendor, all the festivities going on around us as far as the eye could see, and car-riages rolling before and behind (we didn't ac-

tually lead the parade of course, but Lottie didn't care).

Around Parliament Square, up Whitehall, through Trafalgar Square where the crowds were absolutely going wild with joy and cheered us hysterically as we passed, down the Mall past Buckingham Palace, thick with more cheering, flag-waving crowds. My heart was high, I felt so proud—proud of my country and of my little Lottie, riding before me so bravely. For the last time in my life, I was even proud of myself.

I didn't see Maria and Matthew in the crowd, but Lottie spotted them near the Palace, and her little dignity broke and she very nearly did fall off the horse, bouncing and waving. . . . But I held her tightly and all was well. We rode on through the throng to Victoria Station where the parade broke up and my groom was waiting to take our good mount back to his stables.

And our Great Day was over.

I took Lottie home in another cab. What an expense, two in one day! Well, it was only once. . . . She was exhausted, but she couldn't stop chattering and telling me how she had loved it, every moment, and all I said was, "You won't forget it, Lottie, will you? Never never never? Promise me." And she promised.

And when we reached her familiar door, she hugged and kissed me again and rushed out of the cab, and then stopped and came back.

"Aren't you coming to help me tell them, Aunt?"

"No, darling. I'm tired. You tell them for me. Good-bye."

I said it cheerfully because I am an actress. But as I waved at her smiling figure on the doorstep, I felt my heart break.

I made my key that night, as pretty and dainty as the original, and something stronger than I kept my tears at bay so I could finish it off with my nail file, smoothing the rough bits.

And as I fashioned it, I fed into it some of my Gift.

I know now that I did this, though I hardly knew it then—I only knew I was bending all my strength on making the key perfect, and I felt something go out of me, and then the key grew warm again in my hands as if freshly poured, and I knew it had power in it to do more than open boxes. But I didn't know what. I only knew my heart had broken and that I would have given anything to have it be yesterday and not today.

I looked at it. It shone like silver and behind

it I seemed to see the aquamarine drops, frozen like my tears that I had not shed yet. I saw in it a thing of power into which I had poured more than lead.

And when it was finished, I cried at last. I cried myself to sleep. And had a very strange dream that even now I can remember, so clearly that I believe it was no dream. . . . But it is not part of this story. Perhaps the future reader will know what I am speaking of . . .

Maria and Matthew had a telephone now. The next day I made my very first telephone call, from a public instrument.

Maria answered. "Oh, Jessie, I'm glad you telephoned! I wanted to thank you. Our little girl was so thrilled!" For a moment I thought she would relent, but to make matters crystal clear, she said sweetly, "It was the best parting gift in the world."

I felt my heart grow hard again. "I didn't telephone to be thanked. I want to come and say good-bye."

"But—we agreed—in any case, Matt has taken her to visit his sister."

"To say good-bye to *you.*"

"To me?" she said, startled. "But—but Matt doesn't mean that you and I may never see each other!"

"I am going abroad," I said grandly. (Of course this was a lie.)

"Oh! Where?"

"Far away—you don't need to know where."

"But, I do!"

"You've never needed to know where I live in London," I said with a trace of bitterness.

She was silent. Then she said, "Well, come then. Come now. And we'll talk. It won't be good-bye—surely we'll meet again, I couldn't imagine life without you!" *Silly, shallow girl,* I thought. *You seriously imagined you could deprive me of Lottie but keep me for yourself. You want it all, as you always did. But now you'll find everything has its price.*

I went to her beautiful house, where I had known the only happiness of my adult life, for the last time. And there, in her boudoir, I did the deed. She once told me the word *boudoir* means "a sulking room" in French! Is there a word for a stealing room?

I sat calmly, waiting for her to leave me alone. I knew she would. I had arranged it.

The maid who always let me into the house was also the one who would bring us our usual tray of tea. When she had opened the door to me I pressed a pound note into her hand—a fortune!—and said, "Millie, when the mistress rings for the tea, pretend not to hear." "Yes, Miss," she said, looking absolutely dumbfounded.

And she gave me my pound's worth. Maria had to leave the room to find out why no one came when she rang. And in those few minutes I crept into the adjoining bedroom, opened the jewel case whose hiding place I knew well, snatched the aquamarine earrings, and closed it again. Then I slipped back to my usual chair by the window.

I had done it so often in imagination, my heart was not even beating fast nor my breath coming short. I remember thinking calmly, *I seem to be a born thief*. I felt then not one trace of guilt. Not then.

I said my farewells to my sister, quite coolly. I pretended I was going to America. My mind and heart were numb of thought and feeling. The earrings were mine. The score seemed settled.

A pair of earrings in payment for my darling Lottie? Well, I was mad at the time. Mad against my sister, against my life, mad with a grief that, even after last night's outburst of weeping, I hadn't let myself feel yet.

You, reader of the future, before you judge me: Be sure you are not subject to fits of temporary madness during which you may do terrible deeds, with consequences as yet undreamed of.

EIGHT

The Old Bottle

At teatime one of the thatchers came to the window, gesturing. He had something in his hand—it looked like a dirty glass jar.

"Look, Lionel! They've found the bottle!" exclaimed Omri's mother excitedly.

Everyone hurried out into the sunny, reed-strewn garden. The whole team was there, grinning broadly. "The oul' bottle" didn't look particularly old. It was a half-gallon cider jar with a wide neck closed by a screw top, and there was something in it down the middle.

The head thatcher opened it and fished this out. It was a stiff brown roll of paper or something like paper.

"Parchment!" said Omri's father reverently. They carefully unrolled it on the garden table. There were a number of smaller pieces of ordinary paper rolled up inside it.

The parents went quite crazy over these. They were mainly lists of names, and the only halfway interesting thing for Omri at first was a few scrawled comments at various dates, such as "June 12 had to stop work till more thatch come" and "Sep 20 thunderstorm blew the half we done away tarpaulin and all, right across field. Mr. S beside hiself though it weren't our fault" and "Bob T. fell off rooftree luckily on pile of reeds so only cracked his leg." One of the men read this aloud and they all roared with laughter. "Seemingly Bob must've had too much cider with his lunch!"

Then Omri's mother picked up one of the newer pieces of paper and said, "Oh, here's the one from the last thatching, back in 1950!" And suddenly Omri was interested.

"Let me see that, Mum!" he cried, almost snatching it from her hands.

There was the list of names, and a few comments that made Omri's heart beat faster.

"Missus D" (*Driscoll*, thought Omri, *that's her!*) "still gives us our tea though we trys to stop her troubling herself when she should keep to her bed." "Doctor come. Missus D. weaker." And, at the bottom, one last comment that chilled Omri's heart: "We did the last trim very quiet. Finished October 10, 1950. She won't see the job poor lady."

"Omri," said his mother, who was reading over his shoulder, "could 'Missus D' have been Jessica Charlotte?"

Omri opened his mouth to say, "Of course it was," but he mustn't give away that he knew anything, so he said, "Maybe, Mum."

"She did die that year. You know, I've been thinking about it all, since you came up with your idea about Jessica Charlotte living in this house. It's all coming back. . . . I was about nine, and Granny Marie got a letter telling her her sister had died. She was very upset about it. 'She was here in England!' she kept saying. 'So near, so near, all this time!' She'd always thought she was abroad. I remember her crying, which she never did usually, and me trying to make her feel better, and her saying, 'Here all the time, and never a word or a sign! And now it's too late!' Then she put on what she called her blacks—her funeral clothes— marched me into the next-door neighbor's, and was gone for two days."

She broke off, frowning.

"Then something else happened. Just after she got back, the postman brought a big package. I remember her getting it. She tore the paper off it— it was a box of some kind—but she wasn't interested in that. There was a note with it, and when she read it she just broke down. It was awful. She wouldn't show it to me. I remember her sobbing and crumpling it up, and after that for days and days she just kept bursting into tears. 'Oh, how could she! How could she be so wicked!' she kept saying. 'My own sister to be the cause of it all!' And I kept on at her to tell me what her wicked sister had done, but she never would. And after that she refused to speak about her. So I always thought about her as my wicked great-aunt Jessica Charlotte.''

Omri said nothing. He couldn't. He was thinking, *She was wicked then. Really wicked.* But he didn't want to think that. The notebook had said to him, don't judge. He didn't know everything yet. He kept his mouth shut and picked up another bit of paper from the bottle without seeing it.

The older bits of paper that were fascinating Omri's father didn't seem to mean much to the thatchers. They were mulling over the latest bit. One of them pointed and said, quite excitedly, "Here, look, here be ol' Jack 'Obbs, he didn't retire till a year or two back. Still plays a good game of skittles does Jack.''

"And here's Tom Towsler's signature, he's still goin' strong, saw him in the Red Lion last week.''

"I wouldn't say 'strong,''' said another. "Not up 'ere, he ent,'' and he pointed to his own head. The others gave a sympathetic chuckle.

Omri could hardly believe his ears.

"Do—do you mean, some of the men who thatched the roof last time, who signed the bottle paper, are still around?"

"Why not? 'Tweren't much more'n thirty year ago. Tom ent above sixty, if he's that much."

"It's extraordinary!" said his mother suddenly. "They might have known my great-aunt! Don't you think it's thrilling, Omri?"

Omri frowned and said nothing. He was thinking.

"Well, I don't know what you're all rabbiting on about," grumbled Gillon, heading back into the house. "Ask me, it's a dead bore. And I do mean 'dead'!"

After the others had gone off, Omri sought out the chief thatcher.

He was halfway up one of the long ladders. The new thatch had come—huge piles of it, beautiful, golden, and straight, in bundles—and the real thatching work was beginning.

"Could you take me to meet those men—Tom Towsler and Jack Hobbs?"

The thatcher paused and looked down at Omri. "Well, I dunno. . . . Jack's on holiday. . . . I s'pose you could try the Red Lion. That's Tom's local. They got a garden kids is allowed in. If he was there, of a Sunday like, you could have a word, maybe. He's a bit queer in the head, though, is

Tom. You mustn't take all he says but with a pinch of salt like.''

On Friday, school finished for half-term—that was nine blissful days of freedom. No homework need be worried about until the night before school restarted. As soon as he got home, Omri snatched a scone, raced to his room, blocked the doors, and opened the notebook. Patrick was coming tomorrow and he was to meet Tom Towsler the next day. It was more important than ever now that he should read to the end of the story. But he was still only halfway through the notebook. The writing was getting more difficult to read. He supposed Jessica Charlotte was getting weaker and iller.

I went home on the omnibus as if nothing had happened. The aquamarine earrings were in my pocket and I kept putting my hand in to feel them. I had done it. I had taken my revenge. And I could never be caught—never. Maria had left the room for under two minutes, and the desk where her key was kept was downstairs. She couldn't suspect me. I had got clean away with it! I remember feeling madly excited and wanting to tell everyone on the onmibus how clever I'd been.

This feeling of elation lasted for one week.

But it was mixed with another feeling, very disturbing.

I remember that week as one might remember a week of drunkenness or madness when one is not in a normal state of mind, when in fact the mind is not working properly. Later its function returns—one returns to oneself—and looks back in wonder and horror, thinking "Was that I? Was that creature reveling in her vile deed, that conscience-less monster—was that myself?"

And all the time I felt that part of my mind that contains my Gift pulling, dragging at me, urging me to listen to it, to switch to "on" and listen. The strange thing was that throughout the entire week, waking and sleeping, the word "lead" kept coming into my mind. "Lead." "Pour the lead, Jessica Charlotte!" I had a great urge—an urge I'd never had—to cast *my own future* in the lead. It was my Gift, warning me! If I had heeded, could I have changed anything? That is what tortures me.

But I rejected the call. I would not hear it.

Exactly one week after I had stolen the earrings, I left my basement rooms to walk through the streets to the shops. I remember every detail of that day: the weather, my clothes, the look of my hand in its old kid glove as I handed over a penny for an evening news-paper. I remember the newsboy's face.

I glanced at the front page. And there was Matthew.

Matthew photographed on his wedding day, in a top hat and morning dress, with Maria, a radiant bride, on his arm. And before I could brace myself I had read the words under it, the words that burst that evil bubble of elation and shattered my peace forever.

EX-COLONIAL DIES UNDER WHEELS OF CAB

Half paralyzed with horror, I read on. But what was written in the paper was obviously only part of the story. Why should Lottie have run out into the street, making Matthew run after her, straight under a taxicab? It made no sense—I couldn't take it in. *It's a mistake! A mistake!* I kept thinking. Matthew, dead! It was unthinkable!

I ran in blind panic to a telephone. Maria's maid, Millie, answered. She said what she al-ways said, "Mr. Darren's residence," and then burst into tears.

"Millie, Millie! It's Mrs. Darren's sister, tell me what happened, please, tell me at once!"

"Oh, Miss Driscoll, it's too dreadful! I can't tell you!"

"Do as you're told, girl!" I shouted at her down the line.

My sudden anger made her control herself. She lowered her voice, still shaken with sobs.

"It was them earrings, Miss. The bluey-green ones Mrs. Darren set such store by. They was lost, Miss. She couldn't find them. And it seems no one could have taken them except Miss Lottie."

Something seemed to burst in my head. I nearly fainted where I stood. Lottie! *Lottie* take the earrings! What madness was this? My Lottie?

"Mrs. Darren let her play with her jewels sometimes for a special treat. She said Miss Lottie was the only one who knew the secret of the hiding place where she kept the key. She called the child into her room (I was in the room next door, I couldn't help but hear, Miss, really I couldn't!). She questioned her, and poor Miss Lottie kept crying and saying she never took them and Mrs. Darren said she wouldn't be angry if she'd own up, but she wouldn't, and all of a sudden she run straight out of the room and down the stairs.

"Mr. Darren was just coming in through the front door, and Miss Lottie—she was crying something awful, Miss, crying and shouting out 'I didn't, I didn't, I didn't!' hysterical-like, and she run right straight out through the front door under her father's arm, and down the steps into the street! And her father run after her calling her to come back. And then there was a kind of screech in the road as the cab tried to stop, and a thump, and then it was all over.''

I hadn't breathed. But now I did, in gasps. I cried out, "And did she come back—Miss Lottie—is she safe at least?''

And Millie said, "Yes, Miss, Miss Lottie is safe and sound. But the mistress is near to going out of her mind. The doctor's given her something to make her sleep, but God knows what will happen to us all when she wakes up.''

Omri stopped reading and looked out over the garden. The view was peaceful and beautiful, ten days of holiday lay ahead, Patrick was coming. But Omri saw and thought of none of it. He was inside Jessica Charlotte's head, feeling what she must have felt when she learned that by stealing the earrings, she had killed Matthew. That was how she would look at it. And through Lottie! Through suspicion falling on Lottie, the person she loved best.

It was too awful. He couldn't bear to think of how she must have felt.

He tried to read on but he couldn't, partly because he was so wound up and partly because the writing on the following page was suddenly very faint. Perhaps Jessica Charlotte had left the notebook open in the sun, because the ink had faded almost completely. He managed to decipher a few words: "alone" . . . "wandering" . . . "despair" . . . "river" . . . "coward" . . . "never." And then, again, "alone."

He turned the page, cautiously, as if afraid of what he would find there. And he gasped with surprise.

The writing was strong again—stronger and clearer than it had ever been. But it was quite different!

It was written with a different pen, one with a thicker nib, and blue ink instead of brown. It was surely a man's handwriting, sharp, hard, and full of jutting points and steeply sloping lines.

Omri felt almost sick. Someone else had taken over the writing! Had she died—Jessica Charlotte—just at that point? Was he never going to find out now the secret of the cupboard?

NINE

Frederick

I am Frederick Anthony Driscoll. I was born in this house more than fifty years ago, the son of an unknown father. I am a plain businessman who does not pretend to any talent for this kind of writing. I do it only because my mother is dying and has made it her last request.

She has sent for me because she wants this account she has begun completed, and she is no longer able to hold a pen. She says there is no one else.

I am aware of my debt to her, and that I have not been the son she would have wanted. We have never got along. It is a sad thing to say, but it is the truth and she acknowledges it as she lies there. We are different kinds of people.

Everything I write here will be read to her. I am to write nothing behind her back, and add and alter nothing after she dies. This is our agreement.

She asks me to write something of my childhood, but I cannot bring myself to do it. I did not start living until I became independent, when I was about twenty-three. Following my mother about during her so-called stage career, and living, in between, in a dismal succession of sordid lodgings and rooms blighted my childhood.

I acknowledge that my mother made many sacrifices for my education, but the school she sent me to at such expense was—though for some childish reason, I never told her till now—a place of loneliness, hardship, and suffering, where I was brutally beaten for trifles, half starved, and bullied. As for college, I consider it taught me nothing of any practical value. My real school was the school of life and of business.

I entered the metal trade as a young man. I started—I am not ashamed to say it, though my mother, who had expected me to enter one of the professions, was scandalized at the time—as a scrap-metal dealer, later getting work at a foundry, where I soon became a supervisor and later, manager of the plant.

By the time I was thirty-seven I had my own small factory. I made what were commonly called "tin soldiers" (in fact, made of lead) and many other metal toys. (My mother has just drily suggested that I was in search of my lost childhood. Poppycock. I was in search of a *respectable* livelihood.)

On the outbreak of the Second World War in 1939, the government ordered me to turn my factory over to the production of ammunition for rifles. I did not want to do this. I was keenly interested in the toy business. But it would be useless to deny that from a commercial point of view, the war was very good for me. With state money I was able to enlarge my premises. Raw materials were no problem. I had an abundance of cheap labor, mainly women, and once they were trained they were very capable, and patriotically eager to work hard. Of course everything we produced was instantly bought by the armed forces.

By the time the War ended, I was well-off. Some called me a war profiteer. Poppycock again. I did essential war work. Could I help

it if the deprived conditions of my early childhood had made me unfit for active service?

When the government informed me that I
might once again return to peacetime opera-
tion, I had no thought but to go back to man-
ufacturing toys, as I had before. It was not to
be.

I had been so taken up with my war production that I had not kept up with the times.
In particular, I was unaware that a new material
had reared its ugly head, which was about to
revolutionize the toy industry, and bring me
and my business to ruin.

I refer, of course, to plastics.

My mother wants me to admit that my at-
titude to this accursed new material was in
some way exaggerated. I do *not* admit it. I do
not approve of anything, especially emotions,
being overblown. Anyone in my position
would have been bitter and angry to have his
livelihood ruined by this cheap and nasty stuff.

I will acknowledge that I hated it. I hated it
in all its forms, and I never have, do not now,
nor ever will in the future, have anything made
out of it in my home. When I encounter it, I
turn away my eyes. Metaphorically I spit on
it. The only time I ever handled it unneces-

sarily was when, exasperated by my mother's inability to understand my point of view, I brought her some early plastic model toys to compare with those I used to manufacture before the War.

My workers were craftsmen. Each soldier's uniform, gun, horse, and flag was hand painted. The molds for them were made from miniature sculptures, modeled in clay in intricate detail by dedicated artists.

These beautiful and realistic little lead models were heavy to the hand, well-balanced, infinitely rewarding to set up—and to knock down in the excitement of mock battle, when children's voices would bring the little cannons to life, marbles flew for cannonballs, and the bright, sturdy ranks were scattered in a scene of realistic carnage. . . . Those were true playthings, bringing joy and education to a thousand thousand young "generals."

One day my models will be found in museums and be collectors' pieces. Even now they grow rare. They are becoming too valuable to be played with—they must be sheltered behind glass, or buried in boxes and drawers. And those who made them are ruined, cast aside, their skills displaced by—what?

By cheap, mass-produced, ugly, lightweight rubbish. Trash. Cast from carelessly made molds, many of the figures not even colored, their density so low they need no more than a tremble of the floorboards, the vibrations from a child's shout, to topple them. A sneeze can blow them over! Children play with them—yes. They know no better. There is no comparison! I pity them.

My mother has noticed my slight agitation. She bids me be calm, and keep to my narrative. "Tell the tale, Frederick," she says in her husky voice out of her face like a skull. . . . I confess I find it hard to look at her now. She used to be a fine-looking woman.

I have turned the cupboard away. It does her no good to keep looking at her face in its mirror. She insisted on locking it first with that strange little key she keeps around her neck on a red ribbon. . . . She lies now as white as her pillow, the two ends of red ribbon vanishing into her fist where the key is clutched. . . . And there is something else, under her pillow, that she keeps reaching her free hand up to touch. When I ask what she hides there, she murmurs, "The little people." Ah, yes, of course—the fairies! The poor woman's mind is wandering. . . .

Yes, Mother, very well. The tale.

There is not much more to tell, of myself. I went bankrupt, but they could not keep me down. I could have gone two ways—I could have capitulated and gone into plastic toys (never!) or I could have gone back, in a humble way at first, to honest metal. And that is what I did.

I joined a firm making metal boxes of all kinds: filing cabinets, small medicine cupboards, document boxes, trunks for travelers to the tropics, cake and biscuit tins, and cashboxes. I am proud of my products, and in no way ashamed of my life. It was not my destiny to marry and have children. Considering my own beginnings, I am not sorry. A man who had no father to pattern himself on cannot be a good one.

I have read the above to my mother. (After all, a few tactful omissions were necessary.)

She is not satisfied. She insists that I tell about a certain foolish action she persuaded me to. The only irrational act of my life.

I have asked what this writing is for, who will read it. I do not wish to make a fool of myself in the eyes of some stranger. But she has sworn that no one shall read it till after my death. Well then, what do I care? We all have our follies, even the most sane of us. I will do as she wishes.

All my life I have been embarrassed by my

mother's interest in the occult. This fortune-telling nonsense grated on my nerves. I know it paid for my schooling, which made it worse, but worse still was her insistence that I had inherited some of her "Gift" as she calls it— her supposed supernatural powers. *Poppycock.*

After my toy business crashed, a great, consuming rage came upon me. It seethed within me, demanding an outlet. It kept me awake at nights, and even by day I felt it, gnawing on my mind like a rat. I lost weight, I lost concentration, no doctor could help me. And when my mother said she had a remedy, in sheer desperation I said I would put myself in her hands.

This was her bizarre advice.

"You must put your anger into something. Make a container and put your anger into it, shut it and have done with it."

Absurd! Ridiculous! I mocked her then, and I mock myself now for failing to resist the urge to try it.

Nevertheless I made the cupboard.

It was a plain thing like many hundred others the factory was turning out at the time. The difference was, I made this one with my own hands. Cut out the sheeting and welded it and fitted the shelf and the mirror and the handle. My mother said, "Good. But it must have a keyhole and a lock or your anger will escape."

Poppycock! I cannot repeat it too often!

But I did it. God knows why. I did it.

And I brought it to her. And she said, "Give me the key to the lock," and I gave it to her, and what should she do but throw it away! Then she said, "Now, Frederick, scrape your head and heart clean of all the anger that is in them against this material you hate."

"How?" I asked.

"Any way you can," she said.

So I shut my eyes and imagined a pail of clear water. I imagined (what folly! I blush as I remember it) that *I took out my brain* and washed it, and *took out my heart* and scrubbed it, and the water floated with repulsive little globs of plastic in brown and yellow and blue and black. And solemn as a priest, I gathered the awful stuff in my two hands and threw it into the interior of the cupboard.

And though all had been imaginary—I who flatter myself I have no imagination but am a practical man—the gesture of throwing the plastic pieces into the cupboard was real. And my mother slammed the door, and locked it, not with its proper key belonging to the lock I had fitted, but with a key I had not then seen before. The one that she now clutches in her wasted hand.

"There," she said very quietly. "You are

free of it." And she took the cupboard and put it away.

I seem to remember I was ill for some time after this incident. I don't know what was the matter with me. I was weak and sick, assailed with trembling, and I had no appetite. My mother nursed me herself and did not call a doctor. She said it was natural and would pass.

It did. One morning I woke as usual at six A.M. and felt my old self. A lingering loathing for all things plastic remained, and has remained. But it no longer consumed me.

Honesty, and my mother's relentless insistence, have obliged me to record this childish happening.

Interestingly, I recognized the cupboard I had made in the one I found by my mother's bedside, and turned away so that she may not see her face in its mirror. I had not seen it since. But I knew it was the same because I recognized some little details of its making. Some weakness made me unwilling to open it, but I forced myself, half expecting to find—what? I don't know. At all events, it was quite empty.

Personally I have no doubt my own strength of will was the real cure for whatever temporarily troubled me.

Patrick

Patrick arrived at lunchtime the next day.

His mother had driven him to London and put him on the train at Waterloo to travel alone, the first time he had gone on a long journey by himself, so he was full of his adventures, and for some time after Omri and his father picked him up at the station, no one else got a word in edgeways.

"There was this woman, like she had these three awful kids with her and they made such a row I wanted to move but the train was practically full, I could only find a seat in the smoking section. Then I was with these three fellows who were like all swigging cans of beer and smoking their heads off. One of them kept telling stupid stories and

roaring with laughter so it almost made you deaf. The stink of smoke was awful, I kept coughing and after a while one of them said why didn't I push off and find another seat, but I couldn't, so they started trying to get rid of me, this big guy kept sort of moving in on me till I had hardly any room to sit, and the others were breathing smoke in my face on purpose, honest they were like really *grotesque. . . .*"

Omri sat in the front and said nothing. He wasn't listening. What he was doing was trying to come to terms with one of the greatest disappointments of his life.

Frederick's account had brought the writing to an end.

The only other thing that was written in the notebook—though he had turned every remaining page almost frantically—was two lines, in yet another handwriting, quite different from the other two. It was roughly written in blunt pencil, and just said:

"Missus Driscoll died Oct. 30, 1950, leaving instructions in confedance which will be follered to the letter."

There were scribbled initials. They looked like two *I*'s or two *T*'s. Or maybe one of each.

Nothing about the cashbox. Nothing about the little people. (Fairies indeed! That was just like Frederick, to think his mother was "seeing fairies"!)

The "Account of a Wonder" was not there! She had not lived long enough to write it.

Omri had been more and more certain, as he read, that in the end Jessica Charlotte would reveal that she had brought little people to life through the key and the cupboard, just as Omri had years later. He was still certain, from hints in the notebook, that she had discovered its secret. But how she had used it, who her little people were and how they had comforted her, had gone with her to the grave.

Still, despite its cutoff ending, the Account had unveiled a lot of other secrets—secrets he was bursting to share with Patrick. But obviously for that he had to have him all to himself, which didn't happen for a frustratingly long time.

Gillon's friend Tony had already arrived by car when they returned, together with his parents (friends of the family), so they had to have tea in the garden. It was no longer strewn with old thatch, which had all been taken away, but the men were still working on the new roof. Omri's family had gotten quite used to watching them now, but the newcomers were fascinated, especially Tony's father, who was a journalist and part American.

He was full of questions and said he might do an article on thatching for an American magazine, especially when he heard about the bottle. He pored over the photocopies Omri's dad had had made of the various bits of paper. He was quick to spot the possibility that some of the last-time thatchers were still alive.

"I'd love to interview them!" he said eagerly.

"Why not?" said Omri's father.

He spoke to the head thatcher, who said, "If you was to be stopping over, you might speak to old Tom tomorrow lunchtime at the pub. I told the lad," and he indicated Omri.

This was the first Omri's parents had heard about this—Omri had hoped—*private* arrangement. Nothing seemed to be private anymore and Omri gritted his teeth. So much for the quiet talk he had hoped to have with Tom tomorrow. Tony's parents promptly decided to spend the night at a bed-and-breakfast place.

After tea, Omri was just trying to cut Patrick out of the group to get him up to his room, when his mother gaily suggested that Omri and Gillon take Patrick and Tony on a tour. This took ages, because, maddeningly, Patrick was really interested and kept exploring and asking questions, especially about the hens. He was absolutely fascinated about the fox.

"But the henhouse shuts, how did he get in to kill them?"

"Through a bit of a tear in the wire. There, see, where Dad mended it?"

"But he couldn't have got them out through that!"

"He didn't. He just killed three, ate one on the spot and left the others."

"Wow. How did they look, dead?"

"Horrible. No heads. BERLUD *everywhere*," said Gillon with some relish.

"Grotesque!" (This was evidently Patrick's current favorite word.) Then he said, "Hey, Omri, where's your cat?" There was a silence. "Don't tell me the fox got her too!"

Omri said, "I don't know. We don't know what's happened to her. She's been missing ever since we got here." He had a pang of disloyalty because he actually hadn't thought about her much since he'd been reading the Account.

"Tough luck. Sorry," said Patrick. "Poor old Kitsa."

Omri, thinking the "tour" was over, opened his mouth to suggest they go up to his room to talk, when Patrick said, "Did you say the wood by the river was yours too? Excellent. Let's go down there and explore!"

"Yeah!" chimed Tony, and the two of them took off across the yard like a pair of foxhounds on the scent.

Gillon echoed Omri's sigh.

"Just a pair of townies," he said sadly.

"Patrick's not. He's lived in the country for two years."

"Kent," said Gillon. "Flat. All orchards and

stuff, no wild parts. Not Dorset. You can't blame them really."

Omri stared at him. "You like it here now then," he said in surprise. Not much more than a week ago Gillon had still been moaning about leaving London.

"Don't be a dork," said Gillon obscurely. "Come on, let's show them that climbing tree with the old rooks' nests. Do you think Dad'd let us take the blow-up dinghy on the river?"

What with one thing and another, it was bedtime before Omri got Patrick alone. The two boys were sharing Omri's room, while Tony was to sleep in Adiel's.

"We'll have to talk quietly," said Omri. "The walls are very thin, you can hear everything."

Patrick looked at him. "Oh—yeah!" he said, evidently remembering for the first time that Omri had something to tell him.

He picked up the rucksack that contained his few things, mainly two sets of spare trainers, his Walkman, and almost no clothes, and from a side pocket extracted a small plastic bag with some cotton wool inside. Out of a bed of this he carefully unwrapped the figure of a cowboy on a black horse. The little man, seated on the high pommeled Western saddle, wore a plaid shirt and chaps, boots and spurs, but no hat.

Patrick fingered him lovingly. "Hope he got his hat back," he said.

"Remember at his wedding, when he said you couldn't be legally married without a hat?"

The boys stifled fond laughter. "He'd lost his nerve!"

"He got it back again."

"I do *wonder* how they're getting on! Emma thinks Ruby Lou might have had a baby by now."

"Pretty quick if so, they've only been married ten months."

"Eleven."

"Isn't Ruby Lou a bit old?"

"I don't think she's more than about thirty."

"Do you think Boone still drinks whiskey?"

"He said he'd stop."

"Bet he didn't."

"What do you reckon's happening to Little Bear and Bright Stars?"

But for once Omri didn't want to reminisce or talk about their little people.

"Guessing's okay, but look at this," he said quietly. "This is something better than guessing."

He took the notebook from under his pillow and solemnly handed it to Patrick.

Patrick turned it over in his hands, opened it in the middle, peered close in a comic sort of way as if the writing were microscopic, read a few sentences, frowned, opened it in another place, and read a bit more. Omri found his fingers itching. "Don't," he said sharply.

Patrick looked up. "What?"

"Don't just—riffle through it like that, reading a bit here and there. You have to read it right through, properly."

Patrick riffled again and said, "All this? In this tiny writing? It'd take forever!" He put the book down and Omri at once picked it up. "Tell me what's in it."

Omri felt himself getting wound up. He'd been a bit wound up ever since the station, to be honest. This was Patrick all over, so full of himself, and not prepared to be bothered if something were difficult, or took a lot of concentration. But he was Omri's friend in a very special way—he knew the secret, had shared in it, and there was, in any case, no one else he could tell about the Account, with which he was bursting. Besides . . . *Don't judge. Don't judge if you've ever done anything mad yourself.* Omri kept on remembering that.

He sat on his bed with the book in his hands.

"All right," he said. "Only listen properly. It's complicated."

And slowly and carefully he recapitulated the whole story of his find and the Accounts of Jessica Charlotte and then Frederick.

Long before he'd finished, Patrick had stopped fidgeting and yawning and had fixed his eyes on Omri in a way that told Omri he was completely focused on him, on the story.

When he finished, about an hour later, there was a long silence and then Patrick said, "Makes sense. The cupboard and that. Explains why it only works on plastic. Explains the connection with toys. Obviously Frederick was quite hot on magic without knowing it. . . . Being so angry probably made it stronger. Like a curse he put on the cupboard."

"A *curse?*" Omri was startled.

"Well, we did do harm with it. It was you said that."

"But the magic is good."

"Yeah. I dunno where that came from. Neither of them was."

"Jessica Charlotte was! And Frederick wasn't so bad. I mean you could understand how he felt."

"Frederick sounds like a total prat. And I don't see how you can say Jessica Charlotte was good. She was a thief."

"She wasn't! Well, not—"

"Course she was," said Patrick crisply. "She was just as bad as the skinheads who broke into your house."

Omri sat silently. The comparison horrified him.

"You don't understand," he said at last. "I haven't explained properly what made her do it."

"If you steal, you're a thief," said Patrick.

Omri felt strangely upset. "Let's go to bed if

that's all you can say," he mumbled, and stood up
to undress.

The boys got into their pajamas in silence. Patrick
knew he'd upset Omri and was sorry, but he was
too stubborn to take his judgment back.

When they were ready for bed, he suddenly said,
"Let's see the cashbox."

Omri, with obvious reluctance, as if he didn't
think Patrick deserved to see it now, fished it out
from under the bed and unwrapped it. Patrick did
all the things Omri had done with it: tried to open
it, felt the sealing wax, shook it gently. Then he
examined the keyhole.

"You realize the magic key would almost certainly open this," he said quietly.

Omri sat up straight with a jolt. "Of course! I
never thought of that!"

"Pity it's in the bank," said Patrick meaning-
fully.

Omri said nothing. He was thinking furiously.

"There's something I don't get," said Patrick.
"The key was around this Jessica Charlotte's neck
when Frederick was writing. And soon after, she
died. How did it get to your great-grandmother?"

"What do you mean?"

"Well, *she* had it, didn't she? The magic one, the
copy. She gave it to your mum when she was
dying—that's what you told me."

Omri's mouth opened. Another angle he hadn't

thought of. He just hadn't made the connection. Of course the key, and the cupboard too, must have found their way back to Maria after Jessica Charlotte's death, or his own mum couldn't have inherited them.

"Perhaps it was in the will," said Omri. "If there hadn't been a will, everything in this house would have gone to Frederick, would have stayed here until *he* died, which was only last year."

"And what about the earrings? What happened to them?"

"She'd never have sent the earrings back to Maria! That would have been like admitting she sto— took them, and in any case she half thought Maria had died before her."

"Then she'd have left everything to Lottie."

"No, no, you're getting mixed up. Lottie was dead, she died in the London blitz."

"Oh, yeah . . . How did she know that, though?"

"Who? Jessica Charlotte? How did she know what?"

"You said she wasn't in touch with Maria, right? And that Maria wasn't in touch with Frederick, never met him? So how could she have known even that Lottie was dead? The newspapers?"

Omri shrugged and shook his head. There was a thinking silence, and then Omri said slowly, "Or . . . her Gift."

"Her what?"

"That's what she called her ability to—like, know things she couldn't normally know. Maybe she—poured the lead, and found out that way about Lottie, and my mum."

"If she could know that, she could know Maria was still alive."

"Maybe she hadn't done it when she wrote the Account," said Omri slowly. "Maybe she only did it at the very end."

"You said she was too weak even to write. How could she possibly do this lead-pouring bit? It's boiling metal we're talking about, she couldn't even boil water to give the thatchers their tea."

Omri stood up slowly.

"The thatchers," he said breathlessly. "The thatchers! That's it!" He opened the notebook to the last written-on page. "What do you make of this?"

Patrick read it. He looked up. " 'Confidence' and 'followed' spelled wrong. Looks like a child's writing."

"Or a person who wasn't very educated. Wait. Just wait till tomorrow when we meet Tom Towsler at the Red Lion. He'll have something interesting to tell us—I know he will! If only Tony's dad gives us a chance to talk to him alone."

Tom

To Omri's secret annoyance, it was decided next morning that they would all go down to the Red Lion together, for Sunday lunch.

"They've got a good carvery, I've heard," said Omri's father. "Cut-and-come-again, boys, you'll like that!"

"The bottomless plate," put in Tony's father. "Sounds good to me, this country air gives me an appetite." He'd been up early for a walk and to inspect the thatch more closely. "Wonderful craftsmen! The patterning on the peak of the roof, and over the eaves—all traditional, I guess—kind of woven into the straw. Love it!"

"Reeds," said Omri, "not straw."

"Oh, yeah, thanks, must get it right," said Tony's dad seriously, making a note in his notebook.

They walked into town along the lanes between the tall Dorset hedges. The four boys dawdled, picking late blackberries. Omri was quiet while the others chatted. This wasn't what he'd planned. He would have to find a way to get this Tom to himself or Tony's dad would monopolize him. Journalists didn't chat with people. They interviewed them.

Omri had lain awake a long time the night before, trying to figure things out in the light of some of the ideas Patrick had come up with. If what he had said was right, and the key of the cupboard (which had also worked on his seaman's chest) would fit the cashbox, then he might have to break his promise to himself and get the key, at least, out of the bank. He couldn't just leave the cashbox locked forever!

Because it had suddenly flashed upon him what was in there.

The earrings!

Where else would Jessica Charlotte have put them? It was obvious! And this certainty Omri felt about their whereabouts added a bit of ordinary treasure-hunting excitement to the whole business. They were not only valuable in themselves, they were invested with mystery. With history. A family heirloom! And they would belong to him, because he would have found them!

Of course he'd give them to his mother. She had only recently had her ears pierced and now loved dangly hook-on earrings. Omri could hardly wait to see her face when he handed her these beautiful precious jewels.

But it was Sunday. Even if he'd absolutely made up his mind to go against his strongest intention and get his secret package out, the banks weren't open. Good, really. It meant he couldn't do anything on impulse.

The Red Lion had a largish garden at the back, with wooden tables and benches under colored umbrellas with the brand names of drinks emblazoned on them. Lots of families were there already, having lunch, with kids running around. There was quite a festive sort of atmosphere, which normally would have been fun, but just now all Omri wanted was a word alone with this Tom Towsler. A long talk, in fact.

Omri's father went into the bar to order drinks and Omri went too. He looked all around for a man of the right age to be Tom. There wasn't one— they were all either too young or too old. Anyway, none of them looked right.

While his father was occupied, Omri slipped through into the public bar. Here there were several older men who looked like locals. He summoned up his courage and approached one of them.

"Excuse me," he said. "I'm looking for Tom Towsler."

"Don't know 'im," said the man grumpily.

"He used to be a thatcher," persisted Omri.

"You should be outdoors, not in 'ere. What's the world comin' to, kids in pubs, I dunno."

Omri looked anxiously over his shoulder at the bartender. He was looking at him all right, but not crossly. He beckoned him over.

"Looking for Tom?" he said. "He ent been in today. Ent been too well these last months."

Omri's heart gave a lurch.

"He's ill?"

"Yeah, sort of."

"What's wrong?"

"Who knows? Tom's a funny bu—er, chap. He takes funny turns."

"How do you mean?"

"Talks to hisself and like that, if you take my meanin'."

Omri remembered one of their thatchers, tapping his head significantly about Tom.

"But he's not—dangerously ill or anything?"

"I shouldn't think so. If you wanted, you could call on him, p'raps."

"Where does he live?" asked Omri dubiously.

"In the Fairacre Estate with his daughter. She works here part-time, name of Peggy." He wrote down the address. "He'd be glad of a visitor, I expect. Likes young company, does Tom."

"Is this far from here?"

"No! Just up the hill. Five minutes."

Back in the garden, Omri sidled up to Patrick.

"Let's scarper," he muttered. "He's not here, but I've found out where he is. Not a word to Tony's dad."

The address was a council house with a neatly kept front garden. The door was ajar. They rang the bell and a not-young woman in an overall answered.

"We'd like to see Mr. Towsler, please," said Omri.

"You friends of his, are you?"

"Well, no, but we—we have some business with him," said Omri.

She smiled. Clearly the idea of the two of them being businessmen amused her.

"My father's out the back, working," she said. "You can go around the side."

The small back garden was entirely devoted to vegetables, set out in neat rows, interrupted by tepees of runner beans. An old-looking man with a bald head was working away, pulling out spent pea plants and throwing them in a pile. He wore rubber boots and old clothes and had a cigarette end in his mouth.

Omri coughed. "Mr. Towsler?"

The old man turned and stared at them. Omri thought he looked startled.

"Who are you?" he asked rather sharply.

Omri came to the edge of the vegetable bed and put out his hand. "I'm—my name's Omri. My family's moved in to Mistle Hay Farmhouse."

The man looked quite blank for a moment, then a curious expression came over his face. The odd thought flashed through Omri's mind: *He's been expecting me.* The man made no move to take Omri's hand, so he let it fall.

"Mistle Hay?" the man said. "You'm at Mistle Hay?"

"Yeah. We've just had it thatched and we found the bottle. That's how we heard about you. You thatched it last time."

"Arh," he said. He kept staring at Omri. "You'm family, ent you," he said suddenly. "You've got a look of she."

Omri felt his neck prickle. He understood instantly. *This man was saying he looked like Jessica Charlotte.* He said quietly after a moment, "She was my great-great aunt."

The old man gazed at him. He took no notice of Patrick. After a few moments he stepped onto the path and took off his gardening gloves, banging them against his leg.

"What do ee want with me?" he asked.

"Could I ask you some questions?"

He led them to an aged garden table and benches like the ones at the pub. They sat down. Omri pulled the notebook out of a plastic bag he was carrying, and opened it to the last page with writing, the two lines in blunt pencil. And the initials. TT. Tom Towsler.

"You wrote this, didn't you?" Omri asked.

The man looked at it briefly, then back again into Omri's eyes.

"You found more'n th'ould bottle, seemingly," he said. He took the book gently out of Omri's hand and turned it over. "Tarpaulin kept it pretty well dry then," he said.

"Did *you* wrap it up and put it in the thatch?" Omri asked, trying to keep the excitement out of his voice.

"Oh, arh."

"Do—do you know what's in the cashbox?"

"I might guess but I don't know. How would I?"

"I thought she might have told you."

"She give it me. And the book. Told me what to write. Told me what to do—give me instructions."

"To wrap the box and the notebook in thatchers' tarpaulin and hide it in the thatch."

The old man nodded.

They sat in the sunlight in silence. Behind Tom

Towsler's head, the fields, yellow after haymaking, spread upward to the edge of a blue early autumn sky.

Then Patrick said, "Anything else?"

The old man looked at him slowly. "Like what?"

"Did she ask you to do anything, or help her with anything else?"

"*You* ent family," Tom said, almost accusingly.

"He's my friend," said Omri quickly. "It's all right."

"My instructions was to hide one package. And post another," he said.

Omri sat up straight on the bench and glanced at Patrick.

"Post? You had to post a parcel?"

"Arh. A big 'un."

"How big?"

"Big enough to hold what it had to," he said shortly.

"So you know what was in the parcel you posted!" said Patrick.

"Well, I would do, wouldn't I," he said. "Seein' I packed it."

"Please—what was in it?"

"And who did you post it to?" said Patrick.

"That'd be tellin'," said Tom.

"Yes," said Omri.

The old man leaned forward on the table until his face, which hadn't been shaved lately, was only a foot from Omri's. He seemed to be trying to peer into Omri's mind through his eyes. Omri could smell his tobacco-y breath.

Tom Towsler leaned back and said, "I don't mind telling you. Not 'im." He jerked his thumb at Patrick. "She'd-a wanted you to know, you bein' family."

Patrick stood up at once. "It's okay," he said. "I'll go back to the pub and wait for you."

"Don't tell the others where—"

"Course not," said Patrick. He turned and walked around the side of the house.

Omri looked back at the old man, who seemed to relax.

"It ent for strangers, this story."

"Please go on, Mr. Towsler."

He lit another cigarette. "It were like this, see. She made a bit of a friend o' me, early on like, when she could still get about a bit. Before she took to her bed. She set about pickin' one of us she thought she could trust."

"Why did she pick you?"

"It were strange like. She asked who'd like his fortune told. Well, we all did, 'cept one who was 'Oly Roman and said it was blasphemous." He pronounced it "blas–fee–mus." "And it were, in a way! She knew more'n she should've for a Christian, if you take my meanin'. She did some hocus-pocus with boilin' up bits o' lead and makin' queer shapes of 'em in a basin o' water. Well, we had to help her. She couldn't hardly lift much by then. And she told us some things about our lives, and she were so right, it scared us stiff if I'm honest. To me she said, 'You'll live your life alone, yet not alone.' Well! I were well and truly married, had a new daughter, I thought, 'We got a right one here!' But then she looked at me out of them sad, ill eyes and said, 'You will do.' My mates on the team all laughed and said she'd get me runnin' errands for her to the devil.''

"What did she mean, 'You will do'?"

"She wouldn't say, not then. But after the others had gone out of the kitchen where we was doin' the hocus-pocus, she kept me back. Boiled up the lead one more time, and made me steady her hand while she poured it for herself. When I touched her hand like—"

He stopped and looked away.

"Yes?" prompted Omri eagerly.

"I can't rightly describe it. A tinglin' . . . I nearly let go, only I thought, she'll drop the saucepan and the hot lead'll go all over. But holdin' her hand while she poured, well, I wouldn't do that again for a mint o' money, I can tell you. Not to mention what happened after.''

"What?"

"She took one peep into the water and in a second she'd covered up her eyes. . . . Took a terrible

turn, she did. I never saw if she took the piece o'
lead out and looked at it proper, like she done with
ours, 'cause she just pointed with one hand, all
trembling, to the door and ordered me to leave her
to herself. But later we heard her cryin' somethin'
awful.''

''And afterward? I mean, the parcel . . .''

''I'm comin' to that. After a couple o' weeks of
stripping, we started on the thatchin', see, and she
was gettin' worse, with the doctor comin' and goin'.
Till near the last she'd be about, and gettin' us our
tea, and givin' us money for cider or beer. And
times we'd do her bits o' shoppin' for her, till the
gentleman come. Then he took over.''

''The gentleman? You mean, her son?''

''Arh . . . There was no more tea nor nothing
else, after he came, not on the job anyhow. He just
told us to get on with it and to keep our voices
down. And she never come downstairs no more
after that.''

''And did he stay with her till she died?''

''Oh, he were with her at the end, but for the
last week he kind of come'd and go'd. He weren't
there all the time. That's when she called me to
come to her.''

''Called you?''

''Her bed were near the window and we had the
ladders up and we'd look in on her, when he weren't
about, to see she was all right like, and when it was

me going past her window with a load of thatch, she might beckon, weakly, like this"—Tom crooked his finger—"and when I could, I'd go to her room and she'd give me instructions."

"About the packages."

"Arh, them."

"Tell me about—the other one."

"I wasn't to send it till after she'd gone. 'Wait, Tom,' she whispered. 'Wait till I'm dead. Safe and sound—under the ground'—and she give a little wheezy cough and tried to smile. Then she told me where the gentleman had put it away, hidden like. I was that afeared that he'd catch me takin' it and think I was stealin', but I had to do it—maybe it *was* the devil's errand, like the lads said, 'cause I couldn't resist her when she gave an order. Queer sort of thing to be posting. A little metal cupboard. And the key to it." He paused. "And a letter."

"A letter!"

"She told me what to put in it. I were never much on writin', but I done my best."

"Who was it to?" asked Omri, though he knew.

"A lady. My memory's goin'. Whole gaps. Just goin'."

"Maria? Was it Maria Darren?"

Tom's face cleared. "Arh! That's it!"

"What was in the letter—do you remember?"

"It were short enough. . . . Let me see. . . . Something about a mystery—arh, that's it, the key to the mystery. I remember that because she took the key off of her neck when she said it, so I knew it were a real key she meant. She made me write something more about the key, about how it opened many locks—something like that. Then she told me to write three words. 'They're three hard words, Tom,' she said, 'so get them right. *I took them.*' I wrote that down and then I couldn't help it, I asked her what she'd took, and she give me a look that shut me up. Then she said she didn't ask forgiveness because she knew there couldn't be none, and at the end, that sad part. 'Is it any comfort to you to know, my life too was ruined?' I remember that word for word, it gave me heartache, the way she said that, so sorry like, and bitter at the same time. Then she was quiet for a while and I thought she'd dropped off, but she suddenly said, 'Put "love." ' "

"Then what happened?" asked Omri almost in a whisper.

"Then I held the pen in her hand and she signed it with just her initials. She told me to put the key with the letter in the envelope, put that in the cupboard, pack it up careful, and after her funeral to send it to an address she gave me. A lawyer. She said he'd know where to send it on, like."

"And was that all?" Omri asked after a moment. "That's the whole story?"

The old man passed his hand over his bald head and looked down at the table. After a while, he said,

"That's all as I can tell without you thinkin' what they all think."

"What?"

"That I'm queer in the 'ead."

"I won't think that," said Omri.

"Well, then. The last time ever I saw Missus Driscoll—who wasn't a missus, but a miss, so they said, but that's nought to do with me—she give me a trifle for doin' her errand, and she give me somethin' else as well. She give me a present as no man ever had a better, except I had to keep it secret all these years, but for sure that's why I never, ever forgot that lady, and says a prayer for her of a Sunday to this day."

Omri found his mouth had gone dry. "What— what was it? What did she give you?"

The old man looked at him for a long time. His eyes had lost their piercing, steady look and become dreamy and unfocused. When he spoke again it was in a singsong voice as if Omri wasn't there.

"She gave me her confidence. She told me about *them*, and said they'd all gone safely back," he said. "All but one, and she wouldn't go, because she said her life wasn't worth living where she come from, she wanted to stop here, with Missus Driscoll. But she couldn't keep her, like, bein' not long for this world. So she give her to me—she give her into my hand, into my keepin'. And I kept her. I kept her safe, and she was the best friend, the sweetest companion any man could have."

"Can—can I see her?" whispered Omri.

Tom's eyes focused on him again.

"I don't know how or why, but you're the first as I could've shown her to," he said. "But I can't because . . . because I ent got her no more. She lived with me in secret for thirty year, and then one day two months ago she—"

He stopped. Omri saw he had stopped because he was going to cry. He wanted to turn his eyes away but he couldn't.

"She was a little person, wasn't she?" he asked in a whisper. "A tiny person as big as your finger."

"Arh," Tom Towsler said hoarsely, wiping his eyes. "My Jenny."

TWELVE

Jenny

Once started, the old man couldn't stop. It poured out, and Omri sat there in the garden and listened, one part of him worrying about his family at the pub, but that was only a small part. The rest of him was concentrating on Tom and his Jenny.

Jenny had been a maid in a large Victorian household sometime in the 1870's. (*Around when Boone was a boy*, Omri thought. It was hard to compare them, their lives had been so different.)

She'd been put into service when she was only twelve and had been a servant for eight years with an awful snobbish family in Dorchester with lots of children and a houseful of servants. They made her sleep in a tiny attic without any heating, gave

her half a day off a month, allowed her no "followers" (boyfriends, Tom explained), and worked her like a slave from morning till night, doing the hardest, lowest household chores for practically no money.

Her own large family lived in poverty in the country—quite near where they were now, as it happened—so there was no way they could help her. In fact, most of the little she earned went straight to them. She couldn't save anything. There was no escape—this was to be her whole life.

And then one night when she was asleep, curled up against the bitter cold in her little room under the roof, she was transported into a different world—a different time. She found herself in a country farmhouse much like the one she'd been born in, only that it wasn't so poor. And she was tiny, or, as she thought, everything around her was huge.

Terrified at first, she soon found that this was not, as she'd thought, a nightmare. On the contrary, she seemed to be living a dream of happiness in the home of this giantess, whom she learned to call Miss Jessie, and who, instead of expecting Jenny to work for her, did everything in her power to please her and make her happy.

She gave her delicious things to eat, as much as she wanted (the first time in her life she had had enough), and spoiled and cossetted her. She even taught her to read, using tiny cutout pages printed clearly in big, brown ink letters. But the best thing she did was to talk to her and treat her as an equal, as a person with rights and dignity. As a friend.

In the beginning, Jenny was shuttled between her two worlds, and it was like shuttling between hell and heaven. But hell by day wasn't so bad when you knew that heaven was waiting. She began to spirit away things that she needed in that heavenly other place—such as sewing things so that she could make her own clothes, not out of coarse cloth but from the silks and muslins Miss Jessie supplied.

She brought her own eating utensils, hidden in her pockets, and then she grew bolder. With her pitiful wages she bought some cookpots, shoes, books, and other carriables.

At night she would bundle these necessaries up in a pillow slip and cuddle it to her in bed, so that when Miss Jessie "summoned" her (as she called it, as when her hated real-life mistress pealed one of the household bells), the things she needed would go with her.

In the Dorchester household they began to complain about her. She was constantly tired. There were times when she couldn't be wakened. A doctor was called but could find nothing wrong with her.

Eventually, after a prolonged visit that, at her beseeching, lasted several blissful days, she had awakened in the poor ward at a big hospital. The

nurses were bewildered. As she lay there apparently unconscious, eating nothing, hardly breathing, *she had put on weight,* and when she awoke
she was in better health than when she had "fallen
ill."

They sent her home to the family she worked
for, but they were growing tired of her "turns."
The mistress of the house summoned her for the
last time.

"You'll have to go," she said carelessly. "You're
not earning your keep. I'll give you your wages to
the end of this week. But you can't expect a character after the trouble you've caused."

To be turned out without a character was the
worst thing that could happen to a servant in those
days. It meant she had no reference, and without
one, no one would employ her. Jenny left the house
in which she had worked herself to the bone, with
nothing but her few possessions in a little cardboard
suitcase.

Sleeping rough that night in a field, cold, friend-
less, and frightened, she was "summoned," and
that was when she told Miss Jessie very firmly
through her tears of relief that she wanted to stay
with her forever and not go back, ever, to the cru-
elty of her life in nineteenth-century Dorchester.

"And she were happy," said Tom in the end. He
still wiped his eyes from time to time, but it was
obvious to Omri that talking about Jenny had done

him good. "She were happy with the lady, and she were happy with me. It was hard to keep her safe and secret. Any number of times we were nearly caught out. But I worked out ways."

"Didn't your wife—?"

"Left me. Early on. Took Peggy and left me for another man. Dead now these twenty years . . . Peggy come to take care of me after—well. After Jen went, I had a bit of a breakdown. Can't manage like I used to—forget things. So she come. Good girl is Peggy."

"So you lived alone, all those years."

"Like Missus Driscoll predicted. Alone yet not alone! I had Jen. I fixed her up a little place of her own and all manner o' things for her to use, and she lived her little life alongside my big un and we was happy. She loved to read. . . . She used to read to me from them little books she'd brought . . . the Brontës, and Walter Scott, and the poets, Wordsworth and them . . . She loved poetry. Voice like silver bells, she had." He blew his nose for the tenth time. "She was a wonder all right. I been lucky."

"But how did she—you know—die?" asked Omri.

A dark look came over Tom's face.

"She didn't die. She were killed," he said.

"Killed!"

"That's my belief. Or let to die. Same thing."

"What happened?"

"Listen. She were sittin' on my hand, the way she always did when we was havin' a chat. Just sittin' in her long dress, doin' her embroidery. Talkin' to me of an evenin' as usual. And on a sudden she just—lifted her head—looked at me, surprised like, and—stopped."

"Stopped? You mean—"

"I mean she stopped. She stopped bein' Jenny. *She stopped bein' human.*"

Omri looked at him incredulously. "Stopped being human?"

He nodded fiercely. "I still can't believe it, not properly, but it happened. One second it was her, the next second it—she went—light."

"What?"

"Light. In my hand. She didn't weigh hardly anything. And then she—it—it fell over sideways. No proper color. Nothing. I touched it. You won't laugh? It was just a—a brown—a woman shape— only it was—" He buried his face abruptly in his hands.

"Plastic," breathed Omri.

Tom lifted his face. "You know," he said. "You know all about it."

"Yes," said Omri. "I know."

They sat for a while. Tom recovered a little and lit another cigarette.

"What did you mean—killed?" Omri asked at last.

"Them where she come from. At—at the other end, as she called it. Where she'd left—the rest of her. The way I figured it, all them years, she was in that paupers' hospital ward. Just layin' there like asleep, while the real Jenny were here with me. And then one day, after about thirty years of it, well, if you work it out, it was around 1899, time o' the second Boer War, and they must've been desperate for beds and didn't have enough staff, and maybe they just decided—it weren't worth keepin' her alive because like, she was never going to wake up. And that was true. They wasn't to know she was alive and kickin' and makin' me happy three quarters of a century in the future."

Omri said, "Have you still got her? The plastic figure of her?"

Tom shook his head. "You ent laughed so far, so I'll tell you what I done. I give her Christian burial in the churchyard. Made her a little coffin, read the burial service over her, put her a cross with her name on it, this big." He held up his finger and thumb. "Course, it'll all get overgrown in time, when I'm gone, but I done what I thought was right."

Omri, remembering other funerals, nodded.

"Course," said Tom after a while, "I worried

about her. When she were with me. Worried she'd be lonely an' that, for people her own size. But she said not to. She were content with me. She said them others weren't much company. Not her sort, she said."

"What others?" asked Omri sharply.

"The others the lady had."

Of course! Jessica Charlotte had brought a number of little people to life—she'd hinted as much in the Account! All gone safely back, Tom had said, before she died.

"Do you know anything about—the others?"

He shook his head.

"Jenny said they weren't her sort so I didn't bother my head about 'em. The cupboard and the key that brought 'em, they was gone. I'd posted 'em off like Missus Driscoll told me to. But there was a number of 'em, I know that—three or four."

"They must be in the cashbox," Omri suddenly said. "Their plastic figures!"

"Oh, arh," said Tom. "That's where they are, I reckon."

Peggy appeared at the back door.

"Run along now, young man," she said. "Dad's tired now. It's time he was comin' in for his tea."

"It's time I got to work mendin' that roof tile," said Tom, levering himself to his feet.

"You ent mendin' no roofs at your age, Dad.

Don't you be so foolish. Come along in now, it's gettin' chilly."

Omri gave Tom a secret smile, and left them still arguing.

When he got back to the Red Lion it was closed, and the garden was empty. He wasn't surprised. It was well after four o'clock. No wonder they hadn't waited.

He walked home between the hedges. His mind was full to bursting.

Nobody was annoyed with him for going off by himself, except Tony's dad. *He* seemed quite annoyed, for some reason.

"Patrick told us you found this old thatcher," he said aggrievedly. "Said you were having a long talk with him."

"Yes," said Omri.

"What did you find to talk to him about for so long?" he asked, in a tone that implied that nobody but himself had any rights to Tom at all.

"He was interesting," said Omri vaguely.

"I'll bet! You might have taken me along. You knew I wanted to interview him, and now we've got to get home."

"Sorry," said Omri. But he wasn't, not specially.

Tom wasn't crazy, but you never knew. If a real journalist got to work on him, he might have let something slip.

*   *   *

That night, when they were in bed, Omri told Patrick everything—including his great decision.

Apart altogether from the earrings, if they ever wanted to hear the end of the story—to know who the rest of Jessica Charlotte's companions had been, the very first little people ever to travel through time in the magic cupboard—they were going to have to recover the key from the bank.

To open the cashbox.

THIRTEEN

The Fall

"Dad, can we go to the bank today?"

His father continued painting for a moment or two. Omri was standing in the doorway of his dad's big new studio. It was the next day, Monday.

He and Patrick had stayed awake talking for hours last night, and Patrick in fact was still sound asleep. But Omri's brain was seething and he couldn't wait, now he'd decided, and he'd pursued his father out to his studio first thing after breakfast.

His dad turned slightly, his eyes and his mind still on his painting, which was of a large, colorful, impressionistic rooster. Omri thought his paintings had changed a lot from the somber roofscapes and still lifes of gardening tools he had usually painted before they'd moved out of London.

"What bank?" he asked, as if he were somewhere else.

"*The* bank, Dad. Your bank. The bank where my package is."

"Ah. *That* bank. I thought you meant, the one whereon the wild thyme grows."

"Sorry?"

"Never mind. I thought that package was supposed to be kept until your death or something, wasn't that the idea?"

"It was the idea, but I've changed my mind."

"What's in there, Omri? I'm burning with curiosity."

"It's a secret, Dad."

"Oh, okay. Well. There's no problem about it. We'll go in a bit later, eh? I can't leave this now."

Frustrated, Omri drifted away. The studio was in the yard, which was dotted with hens. The five chicks that had been new when they arrived were now half grown. They seemed to be running around squeaking rather frantically. There was no sign of their mother.

He wandered idly into the barn to look for her. She was there, pecking away, perfectly silent now although until yesterday she had kept up a constant gentle clucking to call the chicks to her. She was lying low, not doing anything to let them know where she was. *Nature,* thought Omri. Hens knew the right time to leave their children to get on with it on their own. . . . Did human mothers do that? Would his mother run off and "hide in the barn" one day when the three of them got big and she'd had enough of looking after them?

He was just wandering out again when he heard something. It was a squeaking noise not unlike the one the chicks made. Were there more chicks that he didn't know about?

If so, they were high up, over his head somewhere. He climbed a wooden ladder fixed to the back wall, to a kind of hayloft that was no more than a few boards laid across the rafters. His father had forbidden them to go up there because he said the boards weren't safe. But there was a hole like a trapdoor where the ladder went, and Omri put his head through that, looking for the source of the squeaking.

His eyes roved the dusty space between the boards and the roof. There was no hay here now except a few scraps in a dark corner where the sloping roof and the boards met. The squeaking was coming from there.

If it was chicks, if some daft hen had made her nest up here, they might be killed falling off. There was no sign of a bird anyway. Maybe it was rats?

Did rats squeak? Of course they did, but something told Omri it wasn't rats. Now he was nearer, the squeaking sounded more like—well, mewing.

A dead hope revived itself as Omri crawled cautiously along the boards and reached into the little heap of old hay. His fingers touched fur, warm moving balls of it. He heaved himself closer on his elbows. The boards sagged ominously, but he wasn't aware of it.

There were five kittens, by no means newborn, two black and three black-and-white. One half of their parentage, at least, was quite obvious.

Some deep knot that had been half forgotten in the pit of Omri's stomach came gently untied. He drew a deep breath and let it out on a silent, joyous laugh.

"You fiend, Kits," he said aloud. "Where are you?"

He lay in ambush for twenty minutes. Then she appeared, cautiously, through the ladder opening. She had always loved climbing ladders. She stopped dead when she saw him. He didn't move. Just stared at her. If she'd really gone feral, she might pretend not to know him, might run, abandon her kittens even. Or perhaps she'd fly at him to protect them. . . .

But no. She walked daintily toward him along one board in the semidarkness, head up, ignoring him, straight past and into the nest, where the squeaking reached a crescendo until she lay down in a languid crescent shape and the kittens fastened themselves to her.

She lay there staring at Omri through sleepy eyes, as if mocking him. If cats could look smug, she would have.

"You little beast," said Omri. "You're not feral! You just ran off to punish us, and then you crept up here to be private for having your kittens." She came back for her milk every night, she'd learned to hunt rabbits and keep out of sight, and now she was independent. She didn't need him anymore.

But that didn't make him love her less. He longed to stroke her, but she had a certain look that told him he'd better not. He felt wildly happy. He backed along the boards and down the ladder. Then he raced across the yard and the lane to the house.

"Kitsa's okay, I've found her!" he shouted as he burst into the house.

Everyone in the family was pleased. Tony and Patrick were quite excited.

"Good old Kitsa. Can we see the kittens?"

"Well—I don't want to disturb her. We can't all go up there at once. Just one at a time, okay?"

Tony and Gillon went up one after the other, had a peep, and came down again. Then Patrick went up, with Omri behind him.

"When are you going to the you-know-where?" Patrick whispered as he went through the opening.

"As soon as Dad's ready to take me," Omri said.

"Can't wait! Where are these little Kitsa-cats then? Oh, I see—I'll just—"

It all happened remarkably quickly. As Patrick (who was bigger than any of the other boys) put his weight along the boards, they gave a short creak and sagged sharply under his weight, and before he could grab hold of anything, there was a very loud crack and he vanished in a cloud of hay and wood dust.

Omri was to feel pangs of guilt later because his first thought was for Kitsa's nest. But she had made it where the boards rested on a cross rafter, and apart from the end of one of the boards jerking a few inches upward as it broke in the middle, the kittens were undisturbed—though Kitsa instinctively leaped aside.

Patrick, however, was not so lucky.

He landed first on Tony, who was directly underneath. This broke his fall. Nevertheless he lay stunned on the concrete floor.

"He's dead! Is he dead? He's dead!" was Gillon's first reaction.

"Ow! Shoot! My head!" moaned Tony (only he didn't say "shoot").

Omri jumped down the ladder and without wasting time looking at Patrick, belted across the yard to his father's studio.

"Dad! Dad! Patrick's fallen, he's hurt!" he yelled.

An hour later, Patrick was in a hospital bed after having a broken arm set. He had to stay in for head X rays. He was awake, but dozy. Not all that dozy, though.

"Don't mind me," he said to Omri. "Get it. Then come and tell me everything."

"I'll bring the cashbox here tomorrow," said Omri.

"No," said Patrick. "Don't bring it here. Too dangerous."

"What do you mean, dangerous?"

"Well, haven't you thought? The chest worked just like the cupboard. If the cashbox is the same, and it has got little people in it, when you open it with the magic key, you'll bring them to life."

On the way home, Omri sat in the back of the car, frowning, full of this new thought. The contents of the cashbox were wrapped. He would have to act quickly or the little people might suffocate when he unlocked the box. If they were there at all.

In the past, Omri had usually been careful to bring to life only one little person at a time, and only when he had great need of them, like Matron, for instance, when Little Bear was injured. There had always been the problem of explaining to them why they were here, why they were small, and so on—no easy task. Some thought they must be drunk, some, dreaming, some—Little Bear, his American Indian, for instance—that Omri was a spirit. Later, they got used to the strange situation.

Well. At least these little people of Jessica Charlotte's had been "brought" before. No explanations would be necessary. But they might be anybody, from any time, and there were almost certainly several of them, who, the moment he turned the key, would all come to life at once.

F O U R T E E N

The Cupboard

The woman at the bank said it would take time to find the parcel and get it to the counter. She asked them to come back later.

"Fine—" began Omri's father, but Omri interrupted.

"If we went away for say, half an hour, and then came back, would you have it ready?" he asked.

"Omri, they're busy, we could easily—"

"I want it today, Dad!"

His father shrugged. The woman smiled and said, "That'll be all right."

Omri and his dad walked out into the village square. There was a sort of little house—just a roof on four stone pillars—in the middle, where you could sit. This was nicknamed Georgina after the woman whose memorial it was.

They bought ice creams and went and sat in Georgina. Omri's father was in a thoughtful mood.

"I'm not trying to pry, Omri, you know that's not my style. But . . . Well. Where did you get to on Sunday, for instance? You never even showed up for lunch."

"I told you, Dad. I went to talk to the old thatcher."

"For three hours?"

"Yeah, well. He was very—"

"Interesting. You said so. I think all craftsmen are interesting. They're not necessarily three hours' worth of interesting, though, unless you're in their line of business."

Omri said nothing. The Urge was coming over him. His father was very special to him. It was true he didn't pry. Unlike his mother, who, quite frankly, couldn't keep her mouth shut, you could trust him with anything. Almost . . . It would be so—so wonderful, such a relief, to tell his father everything, and get his advice.

But quite suddenly Omri knew what advice he would give on the present matter.

He could almost hear him saying it. "Leave well alone, Omri. There's absolutely no reason to bring these people to life. Except curiosity. Think of all the problems you've had in the past. Think of the damage you've caused. People have died because you meddled. Haven't you learned anything from all that? I know it's a temptation, but . . . Leave well alone, why don't you?"

Omri bit his lips, clamping back the words that would unstopper the source of the secret and let it all pour out of him.

Perhaps he could just tell about the notebook. He made a lightning review of its contents. No. Hopeless. It gave the whole game away. His father would put two and two together with the time Mr. Johnson, just before the Big Storm, brought Omri home from school and announced, to his parents and to Patrick's mother, that he'd once seen two miniature people with his own eyes. Then the roof had literally fallen in and Mr. Johnson went a bit barmy after a branch hit him on the head, and obviously nobody thought about the business of the little people again.

But just as Omri's prizewinning story had made Mr. Johnson realize that he hadn't been imagining things, so Jessica Charlotte's story might cast a new light on Mr. Johnson's. That, and the cupboard, and the key, and all the funny goings-on Omri's father *must* have noticed last year and the year before, and not thought too much about—then. Now he would, it would all make sense, well, a sort of crazy sense. He would begin to believe it, and

Omri might just as well forget about secrecy. It would all come out.

Well, and why not? It was all over now.

No, it wasn't.

Because he wasn't going to take the advice his father would certainly have given him *if* he had told (and if—a big IF—he could have convinced him it was all true). He couldn't. He was going to break his own strict promise to himself and get out the key and the cupboard and start it all up again.

Not with Little Bear, Boone, and the others. Of course not. They'd been through quite enough, thanks to the magic. But just to see what was in the cashbox. Just to—finish the story.

Half an hour seemed to Omri to stretch to eternity. But at last it was time. The woman at the bank raised one of the grilles and handed Omri the big oblong parcel, carefully wrapped in brown paper, flaps stuck down with brown sticky tape and the whole tied tightly with string.

"You certainly didn't mean anyone to have a sly peep, I see," his father remarked as he signed a receipt.

Omri was holding the paper-swathed cupboard in his arms. Even wrapped, it had a magic feel to it. He couldn't have explained what a huge wave of excitement washed over him as he felt it again in his possession. He wondered fleetingly if people

THE CUPBOARD · 169

who did drugs felt like this. He felt it wasn't good
to be so hung up on something, to get such a charge
from it, to be dependent—to be unable to resist
what you knew you shouldn't do.

That's part of the bad part of the magic, he
thought. *Frederick's part. His—his obsession.* But
realizing this didn't stop him feeling the way he
felt as they walked out of the bank to the car. That
he couldn't wait to be alone with it, to make it work
again.

They drove home in silence. Omri held the parcel
on his knee. He didn't realize he was tapping impatiently on the top of it with his fingernail, making
a muffled metallic clicking, until his father suddenly
said, "I know what it is."

Omri froze.

"I must be stupid," said his father. "The shape
alone—I recognize it. It's that cupboard you wrote
the story about. The one Gillon gave you for your
birthday two years ago."

Omri's mouth went dry. He couldn't have spoken even if he'd had anything useful to say.

His father's profile was frowning. Omri could
almost hear his brain ticking away, working things
out.

That accursed story—"The Plastic Indian"!
Omri'd written the whole thing for a competition,
they'd all read it, he'd received a prize for it. It was
the story that had triggered a memory in Mr. John-

son's brain and convinced him at last that he had really seen Little Bear and Boone in Patrick's hand that day. . . . Could the fact that Omri had done something as solemn as putting the cupboard (easily recognizable in its wrapping—he could see that now!) into the bank vault tip his father off in the same way, that his prizewinning story was based on the truth?

But no. Even though his father was an artist, he was basically a rational man who automatically rejected anything his senses didn't tell him was true. He, unlike Mr. Johnson, had never seen the little people. Omri saw his father shake himself free of his incredible thought, take a deep breath, and begin to whistle carelessly. He had put it away from him. Omri sighed too, and held the parcel closer.

As soon as they got home, Omri bolted into the house, up to his room (through Gillon's, fortunately empty—he and Tony had gone down to the river), where he blocked the door and tore the wrappings off like a madman. The decent thing would be to wait for Patrick, but he couldn't. He couldn't wait! The excitement was rising to a new pitch inside him.

The cupboard, white and shiny with its new mirror and coat of paint, stood in the wreckage of the brown paper looking somehow like a tiny building rising out of mounds of rubble and earth. Omri opened the door, ran his hand over the shelf, and then reached into the bottom and reverently picked up the envelope in which he had sealed the key.

He tore it open and drew the key out by its twisted and faded bit of red satin ribbon.

He could see now that it was not silver, but lead. It was too heavy to be silver. And lead was soft. The sticking-out bits of the key that actually worked locks were getting a bit worn. As he examined them, it occurred to Omri that lead was the wrong metal to make a key from. If one used it too often . . . But on the other hand, perhaps its softness, its flexibility, was why it worked on a lot of different locks. Or, was that just the magic?

Would it work on the cashbox?

Omri fetched it from under his bed. It had got a little dusty. He rubbed it shiny with a stray sock. It was painted black, with gold and red lines, and the red blob of sealing wax in the middle of the lid gave it a bizarre look.

Now, thought Omri. He felt breathless with suspense. *I must act quickly. Lid up at once, ignore the earrings, just go for the little people in their wrappings. Who will they be? How will they be?* And a vagrant memory of a line in an old film he'd seen quite recently on TV came back to him: *Buried how long?* It was said to an old, old man in a prison cell. He'd forgotten his answer, but it wasn't thirty years.

Of course they hadn't been "buried," they'd been living their lives somewhere else.

But thirty years! It was a long time.

No good thinking anymore. *If you're going to do it, do it.*

He put the key in the lock and turned it. The lid sprang open.

FIFTEEN

In the Cashbox

Just as he'd expected, a number of finger-sized parcels lay in the bottom—five of them. The wrappings on all but one were small folded ladies' handkerchiefs that had been white. They were a stained beige now—some air and damp must have got in after all.

Losing no time, Omri swiftly picked up the first parcel. He unrolled it, quickly but carefully. It was like unrolling a tiny rug that had someone in the middle.

The figure inside it sat up slowly, shaking its head between its bent knees. It was a man and he had white hair. Omri took time to notice no more

than this. He was already unrolling the second, and the third.

The fourth roll had nobody in it.

He felt that as soon as he picked it up. When he unrolled it he found it empty, except for some items of uniform. He knew what that meant. It had been the same with Tommy. The wearer had been a soldier who, since the last time he was brought, had died in action in his own time. Omri noticed the uniform was not khaki but red and blue—some older army era. Anyway, there was no point wasting time on that now.

He didn't bother, either, with the last little package. Unlike the others, it was carelessly wrapped in a twist of brown paper, and must be the earrings. Though he was longing to see these, there would be time for them later. He turned back to the little people.

The first thing he noticed was that two of them were men, and one was a woman.

The man Omri had unrolled first was just getting stiffly to his feet in the midst of the crumpled, lace-edged handkerchief. He was wearing rather heavy looking dark blue trousers, a shirt without a collar, a wide leather belt, and braces over his shoulders. He wore slippers on his feet and his snowy hair was tousled as if he'd been woken from a nap. He was holding a tiny newspaper.

The other man was already on his feet and kicking the folds of linen impatiently aside. He was shorter than the other one, very thin and wiry and looked quite a bit younger. His bristly hair was only just going gray. He wore a high-necked black sweater, dark checked trousers, and a cloth cap, and he had what appeared to be a sack full of heavy, lumpy objects clutched in his hand. Where the other, older man seemed dazed, this one was looking all around him warily with quick, birdlike movements of the head.

The woman looked older than either of them. She was plump, with white hair done up in curling papers and an old-fashioned patchwork dressing gown over what looked like a long white nightie. She seemed neither dazed nor wary, but outraged.

"For 'eaven's sake!" she exclaimed irritably. "This is too much, it is really. Just as I thought my bad knee was in for an early night, 'ere we go again, without a word of warning or so much as a by-your-leave! I'm too old for all this comin' and goin'!"

She looked around and caught sight of the older man, who was rubbing his hand over his chin with a just-about-audible rasping noise.

"My Gawd! It's you, Ted!" she exclaimed, clapping her hands to her fat cheeks. "After all these years! Now I know I'm not dreamin'—I'm back!"

"Hullo, Elsie," said the older man slowly. "Yes,

back again, it's like old times. Good to see you. Where's the others, then?''

She turned on the spot, looking all around her, and suddenly she saw Omri. She let out a shriek.

"Eeeek! Who are you!" she yelled, pointing at him. "You ain't her!"

"Of course it's not 'her,' Else," said the older man patiently. "How could it be 'her'? She was on her last legs thirty years ago, don't you remember?"

"Oh . . . Oh, yes. Of course. I remember now. Poor old duck. I didn't half cry after she sent us back that last time, knowing we'd never see her again. . . ." She gave a sentimental sniff. "Well, but who's this one, then?" she asked sharply, pointing again at Omri. "And where's Jenny and the sergeant? And that thievin' little tyke, what was his name—"

"Could it have been—Bert Martin?"

She spun around and saw the smaller man, who had just spoken for the first time.

"Bert. Yes, that was it. How could I forget you, eh, you little villain? You've hardly changed a bit, I'd'a known you on any dark night! Still on the job, I see! No rest for the wicked, eh?"

"Seems like it. My luck hasn't run out neither! I don't go in for climbing drainpipes and that, nowadays. Nice open ground-floor window—nobody at home—no dog—grand haul, easy as falling off a log. Like to see what I got?" With a cocky swagger, he opened the sack he was carrying and invited her to peer inside.

The older man seemed to pull himself together.

"Not so much of your sauce, Bert Martin. I'm here, don't forget that!"

The little man seemed to recognize the older one for the first time, though Omri knew he'd already seen him. He gave a theatrical start.

"Cor, if it ain't P. C. Plod, our friendly local copper! The terror of the night streets, the scourge of the criminal classes! Here—you have a look an' all, why not? There's not a lot you can do about it here, is there?" And he rattled his sack, which gave out a chinking sound.

"I could arrest you, you little weasel!"

"Don't make me laugh! And what would you do with me when you had? You're not even in uniform!"

"I'm retired. But that don't mean scallywags like you can break the law under my very nose and get away with it!"

"Is that so? Look here then, *constable*," said Bert. He reached into the sack and brought out a minute silver tea pot. He rubbed it on his sleeve and held it up for inspection. "Georgian, this is— solid. Bit of all right, eh? I got the whole set here, sugar tongs and all! And a lot more be- sides. Jewels—carriage clock—silver-handled walk- ingstick—got a sword in it, see?" He whipped it out, took up a fencing stance, and made a few passes. "Very nice! Lot of demand among the mon-eyed gentry! Fancy it for your shop window, Elsie, me old china? Do you still have your little antique business in the East End Road?"

"You be quiet, Bert. I don't do business with the likes of you. I'm no fence! Strictly above-board, ask anybody."

"That's not what I heard," said Bert slyly.

Elsie bridled, her hand on her bosom. "What you hinting at? That Elsie Jackson ever received stolen goods?"

"Word is, it has been known."

"I've nothing to say to you. It's beneath my dignity to hold conversation with a petty criminal like you, Bert Martin!" she exclaimed indignantly, turning her back on him.

The little man, whom Omri realized was a bur-glar, laughed mockingly. "Not so much of the 'petty'—not after tonight! Well. If you're all too law-abidin' to look, I'll keep me whistle-and-flute to meself!" he said, and closed his sack again.

There was a silence. Then the policeman glanced uneasily in Omri's direction.

"Manners," he said vaguely.

Elsie caught his glance, and turned toward Omri.

"Quite right, Ted," she said warmly. "We're forgetting. Whoever he is, we wouldn't be here without him." She stepped toward Omri with one tiny hand extended genteelly, the other one nervously patting her hair.

"I'm Elsie Jackson," she said. "Ever so sorry you caught me in dishabil, as the French say."

He touched her hand with one finger.

"How do you do, Mrs. Jackson?"

"Just call me Else," she said with a girlish giggle. "Allow me to introduce Constable Terryberry."

"Ex-constable. I retired in 'twenty-eight."

" 'Twenty-eight?" repeated Elsie. "Oh! Of course, aren't I silly. I'm before you! Goodness, what year is it for you now, Ted?"

"1931," said Ted.

"Twelve years on from us, eh, Bert? And how's the world going then? Go on, Ted, give us a preview!"

"Oh, things is nice and quiet, at least in dear old England. Bit of bother in other countries. Well, you'd expect it, wouldn't you, *foreigners*. But nothing for us to fret about."

"So, it really was the war to end wars that we're just finished with," said Elsie. "Thank Gawd for that!" She turned to Omri. "It's still only 1919 where I live," she explained kindly.

"Do you all come from different times?"

"No, more's the pity, Bert and me's contempor-ay-nee-us," she said carefully. "That means, we're from the same time. Miss Jessie taught us that. Not that him and me move in the same social circles, of course," she added, tossing her head.

"Don't you ever meet—in your own time—you and—er—"

The burglar leaped forward, lithe as a cat. "Not if I sees her first, we don't!" he said. "Seein' she's too high and mighty to perform the introductions. Albert Martin. Bert to my friends." They "shook hands" as well as they could.

"And who might you be when you're at home?" asked Elsie coyly.

"My name's Omri," Omri said.

"What kind of foreign name is that then?" asked the ex-constable suspiciously.

"It's a Bible name," said Omri.

"That's nice. Isn't that nice, Ted?" said Elsie, giving the policeman a sharp nudge.

"Yeah, very nice," he muttered. "Course, Methuselah's a Bible name too, and there's not many of them about."

"Nor Nebuchadnezzar," said Elsie vaguely. "Still. Hamry's a very nice name, almost as good as Henry."

"Omri."

"What I said, dear. Now then. Let's be sensible. There's things we want to ask. I mean it's been thirty years and . . . Well! You can't help being curious! Where's little Jenny?"

"I'm afraid she died," said Omri.

There was a murmur of distress in which even Bert joined.

"OH! Never!" exclaimed Elsie. "I am sorry! Poor little mite!"

"She had a good life. She stayed here, you know."

There was a sudden silence. The other three stared at each other in amazement.

"Stayed here? For how long?"

"The rest of her life. Thirty years."

"Thirty *years!* You mean—small—like we are? Tiny in a giant's world?" whispered Elsie.

"Yes. She was well looked after."

Bert sat down rather suddenly on the edge of the cashbox. "Strike a light. Thirty years!"

Elsie shuddered.

"Like a doll! I mean, I know she had a rotten life in her own time, but . . . I mean you'd be just—just like a *doll!*"

"Wouldn't do for me," said Ted. "I like my independence."

"I was always dead scared she wouldn't send us back," muttered Bert.

"Go on! She wasn't like that, not Miss Jessie! She'd never have kept us against our will!"

"No . . . *She* wouldn't," said Bert. He gave a meaning look at Omri.

They all exchanged glances and then looked at Omri. Their little faces were suddenly pale and strained.

"What's wrong?" he asked.

"You—you ain't going to keep us here?" Bert asked anxiously, all his bravado gone. "I mean—with her—she'd bring us every now and again, but it was only to pass the time like, to keep her company. I didn't mind, once I got the hang of it, but there was never no question of us not going back!"

"I dunno so much," put in Ted, the policeman, with anxiety in his tone. "You remember Sergeant Ellis—Charlie? He was always restless, going on about his duty, how he had to get back to his regiment and fight Bony, and Miss Jessie used to get him to tell her about the war and that—" He turned to Omri. "He was from Bony's time. Napoleon Bonaparte, y'know. And when he'd describe the battles, she'd say, 'I'm not sending you back to that, Charlie Ellis, you're staying here!' "

"That's right! I remember now! There was big quarrels, him wanting to get back to do his duty, her wanting to keep him safe!"

"She was right," said Omri soberly.

They all looked at him again.

"Right? What do you mean?"

He unrolled the fourth hanky and showed them the pitiful remains of Sergeant Charlie Ellis.

Bert blew out his breath in a low whistle. "You mean—"

"She sent him back all right. And he got killed."

There was a shocked silence. Then Ted picked up the red uniform jacket. He lifted it to his nose.

"Damp," he said. "Well, not now. But it's been damp. Look—it's got patches of green mold on it." He touched the tip of his tongue to the stained cloth. "Salt . . . I wonder . . . Remember, Else, Miss Jessie used to tell him, 'There's a big sea battle coming up and it'll be terrible, you don't want to be in that!' It was Trafalgar she meant. You and I knew that. But Charlie used to say, 'If Nelson needs me . . .' "

"That was a victory for us, though, wasn't it?" asked Omri. "Trafalgar? When Nelson was killed."

Ted nodded. "We won, all right, but many good men died to give us the victory, and Charlie—he must've been one of 'em."

"Was he in the navy?" asked Omri.

"No, no. Army. But they always had to have soldiers on the ships. The sailors—I'm not saying they weren't brave—but they was 'pressed. Not volunteers. They grabbed 'em off the streets and forced 'em to serve, and there had to be soldiers on board the ships to make sure they did their duty." He shook his head.

Elsie was straightening out the uniform trousers. "Poor Charlie. He was a good lad. Always cheerful, one for a joke, though not always the kind ladies ought to hear . . . Lucky I'm no prude!" She shed a tear over the helmet and laid it down tenderly amid the handkerchief lace.

Ted was very subdued. "He was Irish. He believed in leprechauns and I don't know what. It was him led us to understand we was part of a bit of magic, not drunk nor dreaming nor dead—"

"That was what I thought at first when she brung us," Bert interjected. "I thought I'd been topped!"

"You will be, an' all, one of these fine days!" said Ted.

"This is the twentieth century, they don't hang a man for burglary nowadays," said Elsie.

"In Charlie's day, they did," said Bert. "He was always on at me to reform, said I'd come to a sticky end. . . . Well. He did and I didn't, which only goes to show."

"It shows the good die young," said Elsie tartly.

"And he didn't come to no bad end," said Ted. "He died for his country. Better love 'ath no man than this." He took a large handkerchief out of his pocket and blew his nose loudly.

Omri said, cautiously, "Could you tell me anything about—about Mrs. Driscoll?"

"Miss Jessie? She was ever so kind," said Elsie. "A real lady. We was that upset when she told us how ill she was, I think even Bert piped an eye when we said good-bye for the last time. Jenny was inconsolable."

"Do you know how she found out—about the magic?"

"Oh, yes! She told us that," said the policeman. "Y'see, her son give her a few little toy figures

186 · THE MYSTERY OF THE CUPBOARD

made of—" He stopped. "What was that stuff she told us, Else?"

"Plastic," said Omri.

"That's it. New stuff she said, and this son of hers hated it because it ruined his toy business and he lost all his money. He brought some plastic toys to show her how inferior they was to the good old tin soldiers he used to make. And she put these little toys all away in the cupboard that we come in. She put them in and she locked the door and said to herself, 'That's where they belong, where he won't have to see 'em when he comes to visit me.' "

"Not that he did come to visit her, so's you'd notice," said Elsie. "Not much of a son, if you ask me!"

"Well, anyhow," went on Ted, "that first time, we—all us five, Jenny and Charlie and us three— we was all suddenly awake in the dark together. Course we didn't know each other, we couldn't see each other, we was just—all of a sudden, like— there. We was a lot younger then, of course. Jenny can't have been more than nineteen, Bert was just a nipper. Charlie'd just taken the King's shilling, I'd been eight years in the force, Else was—"

"Never you mind how old I was!"

"And we was all scared stiff. And Charlie started hollering and Jenny and Elsie was crying and I was banging on the inside of the door, and trying to calm everybody down, and suddenly the door opened, and there she was, staring at us—this big face! Cor, you could have knocked me over with a fevver!''

"You could have knocked her over with one, and all,'' said Bert with a snigger. "You never saw anyone so surprised in your life! Threw herself into a proper fit!''

"Well, after we stopped having hy-strikes and calmed down a bit,'' said Elsie, "we started talking and reckoning it out, what had happened. And she told us this story about the cupboard and the key she locked it with.''

"I know about that,'' said Omri.

"Yes, well . . . Bit out of the common, to say the least, but we had to believe it, because—well. Because it was happening. And she made tea for us and we drank it out of her thimble, which was like drinking it out of a barrel, but she made a good cuppa, I will say that. And we started to get to know each other.''

"Can't say we turned into the best of chinas,'' said Bert, "though I liked Charlie well enough, and Jenny—well, she was a dainty little piece. I could have fancied her if she'd've fancied me, but she didn't. She liked Charlie better, him being in uniform and all that, but what was the use? He'd been born a hundred years too early for her!''

"Yeah, we all had our own lives *back there* to worry about," said Elsie. "But coming here and visiting Miss Jessie made a break, like. Better than a holiday in some ways. She'd feed us special food and tell us all sorts that was happening in her time, or had happened between hers and ours—though she didn't tell us everything."

"No. She kept the bad bits to herself. She never said a dicky-bird about the Great War for instance. When that come along I thought, 'Miss Jessie must've known what we was in for. Too kind to tell us, there being nothing we could do to avoid it.' She was wise in her way."

Omri thought he could stay here listening to his new lot of little people telling their stories forever. But soon enough Gillon and Tony would be back and it'd be teatime.

"Do you mind if I send you back now?" he said.

They exchanged relieved glances.

"That's all right, duck," said Elsie. "Can we go back through the cupboard, though, and not that little box thing? I don't like the idea of squashing into that, all of us together," said Elsie. "Indecent."

"Okay," said Omri.

He lifted them carefully one by one onto the shelf of the cupboard. Bert was the heaviest, because of his sack of stolen goods.

They waved to him, and Elsie blew him a kiss.

Omri turned away to extract the key from the keyhole of the cashbox. When he turned back, he noticed that Bert had fished something out of the sack and was showing it to Elsie.

"Before we part, me old Else, just give this a quick butcher's," he was saying. "If you can resist making me an offer for this little lot, you're not the dealer I take you for."

"Now don't tempt me, you bad boy," she was saying. "Who d'you think I am, Fagin?—Ooooh, look! Look, Ted! Aren't they loverly!"

She and Ted both bent irresistably over what Bert held in his hand. It looked like a tiny box.

"Lovely red leather," said Elsie admiringly, stroking it. "Italian, those are. I seen 'em before—loverly."

"But it's what's inside that counts," gloated Bert. "Go on, Elsie, have a look, a look won't hurt."

"I think we ought to be getting back—" put in the policeman uncomfortably.

But a strange, an impossible idea had come into Omri's mind.

"Let me see that, Mr. Martin," he said.

He reached into his desk and found his brand-new magnifying glass that he'd got for his birthday, for his stamps. Leveling it in the slanting rays of the sun, he saw the jewel case, opened into two layers of trays on minute hinges.

Displayed before him was a collection of minuscule items of jewelry. By screwing up his eyes and getting the magnifying glass focused just at the right distance, he could make out what they were.

Among them were a pearl necklace, two gold lockets, an emerald bracelet, and a diamond pin.

The Jewel Case

Omri gasped.

There was a long silence. The little people became restive.

"Well, come on then, dear," said Elsie coaxingly. "Shut the door on us, send us back—why, look at you, you look as if you've seen a ghost! Whatever is the matter?"

Omri was staring at Bert. "Wh—where did you say you—got these?" he croaked at last.

"Nicked 'em from a house in Clapham," muttered Bert.

"Why did you—pick that particular house?"

The little thief jerked his shoulders once in a shrug. But he didn't look Omri in the face. The other two were looking at him now, and he suddenly seemed to have lost all his cockiness.

"Did you know it was Miss Jessie's sister's place?" Omri asked. "If you didn't, it's the strangest coincidence I've ever heard of."

"OOOH! Bert! You never did!" screamed out Elsie. "Why, you little sneak-thief! You knew she was well-off, Miss Jessie told you about her, you *knew!* You—you took advantage of Miss Jessie's confidence—"

Ted broke in thunderously. "I knew you was a wrong 'un, but I'd never have believed you could stoop so low!"

"They'd treated her disgusting. Made her miserable," said Bert sulkily.

"She never said that!"

"She did. Well—she hinted. Why else wasn't her bloomin' sister around to take care of her when she was peggin' out?"

"But all that was thirty years ago," said Omri. "What made you rob her now? I mean, then? In—what year did you say it was for you? 1919?"

"Because I worked it out. Thirty years ago, when we used to come here before, it was 1889 for Else and me. Miss Jessie was only a little tiddler, ten years old, and her sister, like, she was only a couple of years older. So I had to wait. Till the sister grew up and got married."

"And got rich, you mean! You tricky little

devil," said Elsie. "Biding your time. Counting the years! You had plenty of time to find out where she lived. . . . You must've been planning this one ever since—"

"But how could you rob a poor grieving widow?" asked Ted in a shocked tone. "You know Miss Jessie told us her sister's husband was killed!"

"Ah!" said Bert slyly, some of his former confidence coming back. "I knew he was *going* to be killed—yeah, I knew that! Me, rob a widow? What you take me for? I got me standards! I chose my moment. *Before it happened!*"

"But it wasn't!" exclaimed Omri accusingly. "Her husband died in 1918, just a few days after the war ended!"

Bert turned to look up at him. "You don't know that," he said. He sounded suddenly uneasy.

"Yes, I do, I know exactly when it happened! If it's only 1919 for you now, you must remember—November last year—it was in the papers!"

"I haven't time to waste readin' newspapers—"

"Hasn't brains, he means! It's not that he don't read," said Elsie cuttingly. "He can't!"

"I could've sworn she said—" Bert began.

"She never said exactly when he died," said Ted slowly. "She just said 'after the war.' P'raps Bert really didn't know."

"I never!" said Bert, his voice rising shrilly. "I swear on a stack of Bibles—I thought he was still alive, to make more money for her! Anyway, they're always well insured, that sort, she won't have to stand the loss!''

Omri swallowed. All this was more than he could cope with. But one thing he realized. This was the burglary, and this, in front of him, three inches high, was the very burglar (he had *shaken hands with him!*) that had robbed his great-grandmother of her valuables and forced her to sell her home and later, when she was already old, to go out cleaning to keep his mother.

There, in that tiny sack no bigger than a marble, were all the beautiful things—the silver tea service and the rest, the sword stick had probably been Matthew's—that might have changed Maria's life, and his mother's too.

Perhaps Maria would have had to sell them to live, but if she hadn't, the things in the jewel case should have been Omri's mother's inheritance.

Was it too late?

Could he change history now—the history of his own family?

He crouched down until his eyes were level with Bert's, standing on the shelf in the cupboard.

''Listen to me,'' he said fiercely. ''You've done a terrible thing. You've changed a person's whole life for the worse. Not just one person! Maybe you didn't mean to, maybe you didn't think, but that's what thieves do, they *cause* things, they *change* things. She wasn't insured. You helped to make her very poor."

The little robber shrugged his thin shoulders again.

"I can't help it," he muttered. "I got to live, same as the next man."

Omri clenched his hands.

"Listen," he said again. "I'm going to send you back now. You must go back to that house. You must give the stuff back. Now. Today—tonight."

Bert, who'd been staring at his feet, now looked up sharply.

"I can't do that!" he snarled. "What, give meself away? She'd have the law on me in two shakes of a baa-lamb's waggler!"

"You don't have to see her. Just go to the house and dump the sack in the garden. Or outside the door. Anything. Give it back. Give the stuff back. Especially the case! You must give back the jewel case! Please, Bert! You've got to!"

"If you've got even a shred of decency in you, you'll never know another moment's happiness if you don't!" said Ted.

"I'll see to that, you little tyke!" echoed Elsie. "I'm *contempor-ay-nee-us* with you, and don't you forget it! The robbery will be in the papers tomorrow, I can read if you can't, and if I don't see that the stuff got back all right, I won't rest till you're caught, so 'elp me Gawd, I won't!"

"Else, you wouldn't turn me in, not you! You're no angel yourself—"

"Maybe I done a few things, but nothing like this! Miss Jessie's own sister, fresh in her widow's black, her poor man hardly cold in his grave—"

"She never come to see her—she was no good— she deserved it—"

"Oh! So you're the shinin' instrument of justice now, are you! Don't make me laugh." Elsie turned away in disgust.

Bert shuffled his feet. "A professional, handin' back his loot . . . ! If any of me colleagues found out, I'd never hear the end of it!"

Omri suddenly realized he had the ultimate weapon. Without hesitation he used it.

"Maybe you'd rather not go back at all?" he said grimly.

The look Bert threw at him was one of horror.

"If I give back the jewel case," he whined at last, "can I keep the rest? I got a family of me own! Eight nippers—"

"A likely story!" snorted Ted. "I bet you double the number every time you tell it!"

"I'm not talkin' to you!" Bert appealed to Omri. "What do you say, guv'nor?"

It was all beyond Omri's control. His head was spinning, and he could hear the voices of Gillon and Tony coming across the paddock.

"All right!" he said. "But do it! Swear you will!"

198 · THE MYSTERY OF THE CUPBOARD

Bert raised his right hand solemnly and rolled his eyes heavenward.

"I swear on my dear old mother's grave, I will return the jewel case to its rightful owner, Miss Jessie's sister, at her house on Clapham Common, this very night!" he said in pious tones.

"Now, send us back, dear," said Elsie nervously. "My poor little pussycat will be wanting his tea."

"And my old trouble-and-strife will think I've conked out for good," said Ted.

Omri held Bert's eyes a few moments longer. The voices were close now, almost under the window. "Omri! Where are you?" Then Gillon's footsteps on the stairs.

"Do it," said Omri. "Good-bye." And he slammed the door of the cupboard and locked it.

He just had time to put it out of sight under his bed, and throw a magazine over the open cashbox, when Gillon and Tony burst in.

For the rest of the day Omri went through the motions of normality with his brain in turmoil.

Now—no, then—perhaps at this very moment—no, that wasn't it, but somewhere, sometime, Bert was (or wasn't) keeping his promise.

If he took back the jewels, what would happen?

Nothing would happen the way it did happen.

Maria might not have to sell the house. She

might not have to move to the little house in the East End where Omri's mother grew up.

They might not have been poor.

Perhaps tomorrow, if Omri asked, his mother would look at him blankly and say, "What are you talking about? Of course my grandmother wasn't poor! We were quite comfortably off." Perhaps next time she was dressing to go out, he would see her putting on an emerald bracelet, a diamond pin. . . .

Was it possible that by forcing Bert to take part of his haul back, Omri had meddled once too often? It sounded good, but you never knew. You couldn't know what even a tiny change in history could cause.

Omri put his head on the table and groaned aloud.

"What's wrong, darling? Have you got a pain?"

"No—no. I'm okay." He pushed himself up from the table. "Sorry. I have to go to the—"

"All right, all right," said his father testily. "No need for a public announcement."

Omri went upstairs to his bedroom and sat down where he had been before. Slowly he pulled the cupboard out from under the bed and opened it.

The three figures were there. Plastic now, of course. They were different from the ones you could buy today. They were the same figures Frederick had given to Jessica Charlotte when such toys first began to be made. They really were crude, as he had said—you could see where the mold hadn't fit together properly and the liquid plastic had made a sort of frill all around the figure. They weren't painted or colored, they were just a reddish-brown.

The other interesting thing was that the people looked young. Ted was wearing the uniform of a policeman from the turn of the century. Elsie was a young girl in a long dress with a bustle at the back and her hair piled on her head, Bert a typical burglar wearing an eye mask that he hadn't worn when he was real. But the sack was there, a little rough brown lump in Bert's plastic hand.

Omri set the cupboard where he'd thought of it being, in the center of his line of shelves piled on the bricks. He stared at the bricks. Little Bear, Bright Stars, and the others were there in the hollows between, lying as if waiting. . . . It wouldn't take a second to get them out, and—

But no. He'd broken enough of his promises to himself.

He decided it would be best to keep the three figures of Ted, Elsie, and Bert in the cashbox. He lifted off the magazine he'd thrown over it, and raised the lid.

Only then did he see the fifth package and remember about the aquamarine earrings.

SEVENTEEN

A Sudden Emergency

The second he picked it up, he froze. It wasn't nearly heavy enough. And a faint, living warmth came through the brown paper.

It wasn't the earrings! It was another little person.

He unwrapped the twist of paper in a panic.

Inside was a tiny lady. She lay in the crumpled scrap of paper, apparently fast asleep.

Through the hastily snatched-up magnifying glass he could see her breathing. She hadn't suffocated anyway.

Omri examined her with his eyes, his heart still beating furiously. She seemed to be dressed rather like Elsie's plastic figure, in a long period dress of

a bright crimson red with a bustle and a very full skirt. Beneath the hem her minute feet stuck out, wearing high button boots. There was a big hat (a tiny big hat) with a huge feather plume, lying near her head as if it had fallen off as she lay there. She was holding something in her hand. Omri looked closer but couldn't make it out. The only bit he could see was no more than a tiny dark speck sticking out of her fist.

He couldn't understand this! Who could she be? The others hadn't mentioned anyone else besides Jenny, and the sergeant who had died at Trafalgar.

He put his finger on her shoulder and gave her several very gentle pushes. She stirred in her sleep but didn't wake.

What was he to do? Turn her back into plastic for the moment? Leave her sleeping and risk her waking up when he wasn't there?

At that moment of decision, there was a sudden commotion under his window.

He could hear a woman's voice that he knew from somewhere, saying something to his father in a breathless, frightened voice. Omri left the little figure lying on the table and went to his window.

Seen from above, he couldn't at once recognize the newcomer. But then she turned and he saw her face. It was Peggy, Tom's daughter.

". . . Would go and do it . . . always was stubborn . . ." she was saying. She seemed to be on

the verge of tears, and was twisting her hands together. "I told him not to—then the very minute
my back was turned, it's up with the ladder, and . . ."

Omri forgot everything else and dashed down
the stairs and out into the garden.

"What? What's happened? Is it Tom?" he cried
even before he reached them.

She turned. Her face was mottled red and white.

"It's him all right," she said. She sounded more
angry than anything. "Went up on our roof to put
back a tile that'd come off . . . thinks he's still up
to roofing, at his age, silly old man, and of course
his foot slipped—" She gave a harsh sound like a
sob.

Omri's father said, "Is he badly hurt?"

She looked at him and nodded.

"I'm really sorry. But, er—what can *we* do?"
asked Omri's father.

"I called the ambulance but they said they can't
come for a bit, so I called the doctor, and he's made
Dad comfortable on the floor, like, till they can take
him to the hospital, but he looks terrible, and he
keeps on saying he wants the young lad who come
on Sunday. 'Mistle Hay Farmhouse,' he said, I
didn't want to leave him but he said 'Go now.' So
I got on my bike and come."

The whole family had come out now and was
crowding around.

"Why does he want you, Omri?" asked his father in an odd voice. "Why you?"

"Got something to tell him, seemingly," said Peggy. "Please, do come, it'll put his mind at peace."

"But he's—he's not going to die, is he?" asked Omri.

Peggy only stared at him with her mouth open.

Omri's father said, "Just let me turn the car around in the lane, and we'll take you home. Leave the bike here."

Tom was lying on the living room floor of the little house, his head turned to face the open door. As soon as Peggy pushed Omri in ahead of her, the old man's face seemed to change.

"I remembered," he croaked out. His face twisted with pain.

"How are you, Dad?" Peggy asked.

Tom groaned for answer.

"They'll be comin' soon," she said comfortingly. She gave Omri another little push. "Go and speak to him," she whispered. "Don't be frightened."

Omri hadn't realized he was frightened, but he was. Tom looked really bad. His face was contorted and there was a big black lump on one side of it. There was a bad smell in the room, and as Omri slowly approached, he saw that Tom had been sick.

Omri tried to ignore that. He knelt down beside Tom, who was lying on a folded blanket, avoiding the mess as well as he could. The old man moved his hand as if he wanted Omri to put his own hand into it, but somehow Omri couldn't. It was hard enough, just looking at that hurt, swollen face.

"I done for m'self this time," muttered Tom. "Should've listened. Poor Peg. Old fool, me. Right on my silly head."

"Why—what did you want to tell me, Mr. Towsler?"

Tom moved his head a little, and winced. "Get them others out. Her too."

Omri looked over his shoulder. Peggy and his father were in the doorway. Peggy looked baffled.

"I got to clean you up, Dad."

"Not now! Go out. Good girl."

Omri's father touched Peggy's arm. They went out and shut the door.

Tom's hand, rough and rather dirty, had crept to Omri's shirt. Now it clutched it and pulled his face down.

"I remembered. As I fell, like. There was somethin' else."

Omri stared into his eyes. He didn't know if he was really dying, but he looked very strange, quite different from before. Omri could hardly breathe, not just for the bad smell but for fear. He had never been so close to someone badly hurt.

Tom's voice came out in jerks.

"She told me. What she wanted. It was hard. Hard to find it. Shops . . . Local no use. Too small, see. Take the bus, she said. Dorchester. No good again. Too small. Came back. Told her. She give me money. London. Train. All that way . . . First time, me! Had to ask . . . big shops . . ."

He closed his eyes and his head rolled over toward the floor. Omri could only watch, helplessly. The rough hand had released his shirt, but he couldn't lean back because when the words started again, he could barely hear.

"Bought dozens of 'em," Tom said. "How could I know . . ."

"Dozens? Of what?" Omri asked sharply.

The urgency in his voice seemed to recall Tom to consciousness, from wherever he was slipping away to. His head jerked, his eyes opened. He grasped Omri again and now his eyes were piercing.

"Brought 'em back in a box," he said with a strange, grim urgency as if giving him a vital message. "Showed 'em to her when she—on her own—she looked at 'em all—picked one. Is that the one? I said. Yes, she said. I'll throw the others out, I said. Then she give, like, a cry. No, she said. Don't do that. Take care of 'em. This one's me but everyone is someone."

Omri stiffened and straightened his back. His eyes were wide open.

The old man's head rolled on the floor again. Omri bent to hear him, but all he said was, "On my way, Jen."

The ambulance came while they were still there and Tom was lifted gently onto a stretcher and carried out to it. Peggy was trying to clean up and put on her coat to go with him, and pay some attention to her "guests," all at the same time. She was in a state and Omri's father told her not to bother, just to go to the hospital with her father.

"In fact we'll take you," he added. "We've got a friend there who has to be brought home today."

"I'd prefer to go with him in the ambulance," said Peggy.

On the drive to the hospital, Omri's father kept glancing at Omri's taut face.

"I don't like all this, Omri," he said suddenly. "I thought it was all a game at first. But I'm beginning to think it's a good deal more than that."

Omri said nothing. He felt panicky.

"Are you in some kind of trouble?"

"No, Dad. I'm fine."

His father seemed about to ask more. But then he turned back to face the road. They finished the drive in silence.

When they got to the hospital and parked, his father said, "Is Patrick in on this, whatever it is?"

Omri said, "It's nothing, Dad. There's nothing to be in on."

"Don't lie to me, bubba," said his father quietly. He only called the boys "bubba" when he was feeling something very strong for them.

Omri felt more panicky then ever, though he didn't quite know why.

Patrick was full of bright chat about his fellow patients all the way home. Omri kept quiet, thinking, thinking . . . There was no time, when they got back, to tell Patrick any of the awful lot that had happened meanwhile. He just dragged him up the stairs to his room.

"Block the doors," he said. "Now look."

He showed the still sleeping lady to Patrick.

"She looks a bit like Ruby Lou," said Patrick.

"She's years later than Ruby," said Omri. "And a different country." He was staring at her.

"Who do you suppose she is?" Patrick asked.

"I don't suppose. I know who she is," said Omri. Patrick looked at him.

"How can you? Who is she, then?"

"She's Jessica Charlotte," said Omri.

EIGHTEEN

The Sleeping Lady

"*Jessica Charlotte!*"

"Keep your voice down. Yes."

"How can it be? She put these figures in here!"

"Yes. And she put one in for herself as well."

Patrick gaped at him. "She—she wanted someone to find it, and—and bring her back!"

"Well, wouldn't you? It's a way of not being absolutely dead."

"No—no—my mind's *boggling*—hang on!"

"She sent Tom Towsler to London to comb the toy departments for figures that could be her. She chose the one she felt right about. Her Gift helped her to pick, of course. Then she put it in the cashbox with the others, knowing that if, in the future, any-one brought them to life, she'd come to life too.''

"Omri, shut up, this is impossible! Wait. If she was brought, I mean like now, it must have been during her lifetime. She would know. She'd re-member coming!"

"She did."

"What? You didn't tell me that!"

"I forgot. It was just a little thing, part of the Account that you couldn't be bothered to read. Here, I'll find it!"

He unearthed the notebook, leafed through the pages, and found the place he wanted.

"Here it is! It came back to me when Tom told me. Now listen! It was on the night she made the key. '. . . I cried myself to sleep. And had a very strange dream that even now I can remember, so clearly that I believe it was no dream. . . . But it is not part of this story. *Perhaps the future reader will know what I am speaking of . . .'* "

Omri looked up at Patrick. His eyes were blazing. Then he pointed to the sleeping lady.

"Look! There she is, asleep. She didn't even un-dress, just fell asleep where she was . . . I know what that little thing in her hand is, see it just sticking out? It's the key, of course! She's just fin-ished making it!"

"The key . . ." said Patrick in a dazed way.

"We've brought her right in the middle of her story, don't you see! If we could wake her now, for her to have her 'dream,' which is really coming *here*, we might be able to persuade her not to steal the earrings!"

Patrick was perfectly still and silent for a long moment. Then he put both hands up to his ears and pressed hard. He pressed so hard he was shaking all over and his face was contorted worse than Tom's.

Then he dropped his hands and looked Omri in the face.

"You are raving mad," he said between his teeth. "This is dangerous. You always used to tell me I didn't think but just went ahead and did stuff, but you're ten thousand times worse!"

"What are you—?"

"You refused to bring Little Bear and the others back because you said it was dangerous and not a game, but this is far, far worse. You don't know what you're playing with here. If you change what happened, what we know happened—if that's possible—your whole life could be knocked crooked. You could turn into a different person. *It could turn out that you weren't even born.*"

Omri said "What?" as if he hadn't heard properly.

"Listen, listen to me!" Patrick sounded frenzied. "So in a few minutes she wakes up, and you talk to her, and you change it. She goes back, and decides not to steal the earrings, because you talked her out of it in her 'dream.' So she doesn't. So Maria doesn't suspect Lottie, who doesn't run out the door, Matthew doesn't run after her, *he isn't killed.* He lives to be old, he goes on earning, maybe he goes abroad again, or they move house—anyway, their whole lives are different. So it's very likely that Lottie doesn't meet your mum's father, so your mum won't be born. So you won't be born. That's just one of the million things that would be changed just because Jessica Charlotte decides not to steal the earrings!"

Yes, thought Omri. Something like a blinding flash had come to him while Patrick was speaking. *Yes, that's what I was worrying about about the jewel case, but I couldn't figure it out.* He was staring at Patrick when his face seemed to blur and darken. The suppressed panic Omri had been feeling all day suddenly loomed up like a wave three times his own height and threatened to swamp him. *The jewel case. The jewel case. Bert was taking back the jewel case!* That would change everything just as much! Maybe in a few minutes or hours, Omri would just—disappear!

Patrick was still talking.

"Let's put her back into the cupboard, or the cashbox," he was saying. "Turn the key, send her back—"

Omri wrenched himself away from his terrifying thoughts.

"But her dream," he said slowly. "She had her dream. If we send her back, it won't happen. And it did happen. We've got to let her wake up here, and have her dream."

Patrick said nothing for a moment. He was breathing hard. "Right," he said. "You're right. She wakes up, she talks to us, she goes back. *But we don't try to talk her out of stealing the earrings.* We don't even know about the earrings. We just talk to her a bit and then she goes back and everything happens the way it did happen, and it'll be all right."

"No," said Omri, "it won't. It's too late. I've done something—"

They were interrupted by a little sound like a moan.

They turned. The sleeping lady had woken, and was sitting up. She was staring at the key in the palm of her hand.

Omri sat down at his desk and leaned so that his face was level with hers.

"Hallo," he greeted her softly.

She looked up at him, gasped, and jumped to her feet.

She was about forty, and not pretty. She was little and rather dumpy. But she had a strong, determined face, and a mass of brown curly hair piled onto her head. With her red dress (the very one she had worn at the parade, Omri remembered now) swirling around her, she looked rather glamorous and dashing. He knew right away that if he were only to have the chance and despite all he knew, he could like her.

"Where am I?" she cried. Then she saw him properly, and raised both hands to her mouth to keep back a scream.

"You're having a dream," said Omri. "Look out. You—you've dropped the key."

Jessica Charlotte looked around wildly, stooped, searched amid the paper creases, and then snatched something up.

"My key!" she exclaimed. "I mustn't lose my key!"

"Perhaps you could thread it on a ribbon and hang it around your neck," suggested Omri. He felt as if he too were in a dream, as if the words he was speaking were lines in a play written and performed long ago.

She stared at him, trembling. "Thank you," she said. "What a good idea." She examined her wide sleeve, pulled a bow loose, and drew a red ribbon out of its eyelet holes around her sleeve. She threaded it through the top of the key, tied the two ends together, and slipped it around her neck.

"So you enjoyed the parade," said Omri. "I wish I could have seen it."

She looked at him in bewilderment. "You—you weren't there?" she asked. "Everyone was there!"

"Not me."

"How do you know—I rode in the parade?" she asked him.

"I just do," said Omri. "Don't worry about it. Dreams don't have to make sense."

She was staring at him. "Are you related to me?" she asked.

"I'm your—I'm your posterity," Omri said solemnly.

"Are you Fred's son?"

"If you'd ever poured the lead for him, you'd know he never had a son," Omri said.

"Shall I pour the lead for you?" she asked, still gazing at him.

"But you haven't got any lead here."

"I have the key!" she said with sudden gaiety, holding it up. "Shall I melt this down, and read your fortune?"

Omri gave Patrick a swift look. Patrick shook his head violently. Omri looked back at the lady.

"You'd melt the key down—lose it?"

"I could make another!" she said, and tossed her head. "Come. Let's do it. I'll tell you everything."

"No," said Omri. "I don't want to know the future."

She stopped smiling.

"Oh, wise young man," she said softly, "how I do honor thee!"

Then Omri heard himself say, "I could tell you your future, though."

Patrick trod heavily on his foot under the desk. The lady said, "Have you inherited my Gift?"

"No," said Omri. "I just have an open mind."

"An open mind . . . an excellent attribute! I must remember that—'an open mind.' Tell me just one thing," she said. "Only one. If you know it . . . Truthfully. Will you?"

There was silence in the room. Then Omri nodded. He couldn't help himself. The knowledge he had of her was bursting in his mouth.

"Will I do what I have set myself to do?"

"Yes," said Omri. "You'll do it."

"And will I live to be glad, or to regret . . . ?"

Before Omri could say a word, Patrick had pushed him aside.

"Miss Driscoll! Could you sing one of your songs for us?"

"One of my—oh! It's been months since I've performed. I have nothing prepared—"

"Oh, please! We've never been to the music halls."

"Never been! Oh, then, even in a dream, I must oblige you, young sirs!"

Her manner had changed. She put a hand up to

her hair, then looked about her, saw her hat lying near her feet, and swooped to pick it up. She turned her back for a moment and set it on her pile of hair, thrusting two almost invisible hatpins through the crown to hold it in place. Then she turned to face them.

"I need a stage!" she cried loudly.

Omri looked around. The cashbox! He turned it upside down so that its smooth metal base, with no lump of sealing wax or little curved handle to trip her, was on top. He opened a book and stood it behind the platform like scenery.

With his good hand—the other arm was in a cast—Patrick turned the desk lamp so that it shone on the stage, and switched it on. A big school eraser provided a convenient step. In a moment the little crimson-red figure in the big, plumed hat had mounted the small platform—just the right size for her. She seemed to become an *artiste* before their eyes. Her plump little figure grew taller, more commanding.

"Ladies AND gentlemen!" she cried, thrusting out her arms to them as if they were a huge audience. Her face was smooth and smiling—there was no sign of trembling now! "Tonight I have no one to announce me, so I must announce myself! Well, I've always wanted to—those announcers, they never say what we wish they would! Who knows the worth of an *artiste* better than she does?"

She gave a cocky little flick of her head that made them laugh out loud.

"Nor do I have an accompanist. But do I need one? NO! I have a voice that will carry to the back of any gallery in England, or any barrack, come to that! Sit back, ladies and gentlemen, and enjoy the entertainer who has thrilled the crowned heads of Europe and cheered the troops on their way to fight the foe! I give you—the darling of the halls—the toast of the tommies—Miss JESSIE DRISCOLL!"

The boys burst into spontaneous applause, Omri clapping and Patrick slapping his good hand on his knee. They couldn't help it. She acknowledged it, then held up her hands. When they were perfectly quiet, she began to sing, her clear tones ringing out as if amplified:

"There's no one that you'd rather see—than me!
There's no one that I'd rather be—than me!
Though I'm not one to boast, you should know
  I'm the toast
Of London and Brum and each town on the
  coast!

"My admirers I don't count in scores, no siree,
They flock in their hundreds and hoards, you
  see!
I live for applause and I'm waiting for yours—
For the modestest girl on the boards!!"

She dipped and swirled and smiled and swayed, primping as if before a mirror and then turning to wink at them, involving them in the joke. There were a lot more verses, full of delicious barefaced conceit, and all such fun that the boys sat enchanted, all else forgotten. She made them join in the chorus and refused to accept it until it was loud enough, so in the end they were shouting out "I'm the modestest girl on the boards!" at the tops of their voices.

When she finally finished—in a last twirl, and a deep, deep curtsey with arms again outstretched—they burst into applause and cheers.

"That was terrific! Thanks! Thank you so much!" they cried, and Patrick added, "Well, now we've seen music hall, and it's every bit as good as—"

"What *are* you doing? Who've you got in there?"

The voice came from the other side of the door, which began moving inward against the pile of bricks. The two boys froze.

"Quick! It's Gillon!" hissed Omri.

Patrick, who was fractionally nearer than Omri, snatched Jessica Charlotte up in his hand, upended the cashbox, thrust her into it, and slammed it shut.

"The key! Where's the key!"

"Here!"

They turned it, just as Gillon and Tony came

pushing their way in, the bricks sliding across the floorboards.

"Have you got a radio in here?" asked Tony, looking around.

"Hey, Ton'," said Patrick. "I'm back! Aren't you going to ask me how I am?"

"Oh, yeah! How are you? Who was singing?"

"We were," said Omri.

"Yeah, but someone else was as well, a tiny little squeaky voice."

"It wasn't—" began Omri, but Patrick nudged him and said, "That was me. You want to hear me sing a music hall song?"

The other two boys gaped at him. "A what song?"

"A song from the old music hall. I—I learned it from an old boy in the hospital who used to be on the—on the boards. Listen!" And he began to sing in a fair imitation of Jessica Charlotte's high-pitched little-big voice.

"My admirers I don't count in scores, he-he—"

The other two roared and groaned and held their ears.

"What kind of garbage is that?" said Gillon. "Knock it off! Come on, Mum's going to take us to the wildlife park!"

NINETEEN

Maria's Bequest

It should have been a wonderful afternoon out. The wildlife park was part of a local country estate, where they also made the most delicious ice cream. There was a really good adventure playground there too, as well as a nature trail, and the animals included elephants and a rhino.

Gillon and Tony had a whale of a time. They couldn't understand why Omri and Patrick were so down. They soon took off on their own and weren't seen again till teatime.

Omri had got Patrick alone outside the big cats' area early on, and told him what he'd done. Patrick hadn't been much comfort.

"None of the mad things I did last year were

half as mad as that," was all he could find to say. "We'll have to hope this Bert bottles out of it."

"He swore on his mother's grave!"

"Big deal. He probably doesn't even know where it is. Obviously about as trustworthy as a sewer rat."

"Do you think I should have brought him back and told him not to bother?"

"I don't know. It's all too much for me. I wish we could just forget it now and enjoy this!" They stared at a leopard for a while. It was lying motionless in the grass about fifty yards beyond the fence. It didn't look at all dangerous, as if you could just go up and stroke it and it would purr.

"Wasn't she terrific, though—your Jessica Charlotte," said Patrick.

"Yes," said Omri.

"You'd never think she was a thief."

"You shouldn't judge, if you've ever done anything mad yourself," said Omri. "And you have and so have I."

Patrick looked around at him. "Did you think of that?"

"No. It's in the Account."

"I think I'll read that after all," Patrick said. "Now I've met her. She seemed like . . . quite a woman. Pity we can't bring her back for an encore!"

"Or just to talk to her."

"Yeah." He straightened up. "Hey, I could mur-
der an ice cream. I'm going back to the shop. D'you
want me to bring you one?"

"Yes. No. I dunno. No, don't bother. See you
later."

Patrick dashed off, and Omri went the other way.

The jewel case . . . it all hung on that! If only
he knew! . . . Something about the jewel case was
tickling the back of his mind, something reassuring,
if he could only think of it . . . but it eluded him.
He felt a shadow hanging over him that he couldn't
get out from under.

He thought that no one in the world before him
had had to worry that at any time he could not just
disappear but *never have been*. No. Surely that
couldn't happen. Could it? Time was so weird, so—
ungraspable. Clocks and watches made it seem sim-
ple but it was just like with these animals. You put
fences around them and thought you had them
tamed but there was so much more to them than
that. You couldn't tame time.

He saw his mother at a distance and swerved to
walk toward her. She was standing close to a high
mesh fence.

"I hate monkeys," she said, gazing intently at a
group of baboons. Most of them were picking fleas
out of each other's fur, but two big males suddenly

began jumping up and down, snarling and screech-
ing. The mother baboons snatched up their babies
and scattered.

"So why aren't you looking at some other animal, like the giraffes? You like giraffes."

"Only because of their crazy-paving coats," she
said obscurely. "Look at those urky beasts, how
disgustingly like us they are! I wish they were all
in Africa."

"I wish we were too!" said Omri fervently. Although it wouldn't make any difference to his anxiety. If it turned out he'd never been born, he could
just as easily disappear in Africa as here.

"Have you seen the bison?" his mother asked.

"Are there bison? I'd like to see those," said
Omri. He always liked anything that reminded him
of American Indians, although Little Bear's tribe
was not from the plains and didn't hunt buffalo.

They wandered off to another part of the park.
It was a lovely afternoon. The English countryside
stretched away on all sides, with the strangeness
of wild animals from faraway countries dotted
about in it. A herd of zebra grazed on a green hill,
and you could hear the screech of peacocks from
near the big house.

Omri had a strong urge to put his hand into his
mother's, but he thought it would look babyish.
He just needed to hang onto her, suddenly. There
was so much fear inside him.

"Mum."

"Mm?"

"Are you sure you grew up in the East End? Are you sure your gran was poor?"

She looked at him, puzzled. "What a funny question! Did you think I was making it up?"

Bert hasn't done it yet, Omri thought. Well, it was only a few hours since he'd sent them back. If only the little burglar decided to break his solemn vow! If only he just kept the swag, like a good thief!

But then he might be afraid Omri would bring him back. Of course he could do that. But somehow Omri felt a deep reluctance to bring any of the three of them back again. It was as if he'd burned his fingers last time he'd touched them and now he was afraid, in a very deep place inside, to touch them again. Of course Bert couldn't know that, so he might do what he'd promised just in case. Or because he was afraid of Elsie turning him in . . .

"Mum," Omri said. "You know the red leather jewel case that my key belonged to."

"Yes."

"Funny that when that was stolen, the burglar left the key behind."

"But he didn't. The key was in the lock that night. Nice work, eh? Meant he didn't even have to break the box to get at the jewels."

"But—but—but you said Maria left *you* the

key—for—for your legacy? The one you gave me?"

"No, no, that wasn't that one! That was a spare."

"Is that what she told you? That she'd had a spare key?"

His mother had a funny look. Her eyes had gone narrow, as if she were watching something.

"Come to think of it . . ."

"What?"

"When she was dying . . . she called it 'Jessie's key.' She said . . ." She stopped. She stopped walking too, as if to help her concentrate.

"*What*, Mum?" Omri almost shouted.

"Omri, don't . . . Don't yell at me now . . . I'm trying to remember. She was so pitiful . . ." Suddenly she began to cry.

"Mum!" Omri burst out, shocked.

"I'm sorry." She tried to pull herself together, blowing her nose. "You see, I never knew my mother. I was only a baby when she was killed by a bomb. And Daddy was killed in the navy, at the battle of St. Nazaire. Granny Marie was the only real family I had. I loved her so very much, and she loved me. I was all she had left too."

Omri said nothing. Slowly his mother began to walk again, and he kept beside her. Something was coming out of her deepest memory, something very, very important to him.

"She was quite well, till near the end, and then

she suddenly had a heart attack. She was taken into
the hospital. Adiel was only about a month old at
the time. I was running to and fro like mad, to visit
her. I felt frantic. I knew she was going to die—
she was in her eighties—and I couldn't bear it
somehow. I wanted her to live forever. . . . And
she was so distressed, so upset, and I couldn't find
out what was bothering her. I wanted her at least
to die in peace. And then at last, she came out with
it."

"What?"

She walked for a long time in silence. His im-
patience was almost too much to bear, but he did
bear it.

"Simply that she had nothing to leave me. I
couldn't believe it! As if I cared! And that was when
she started going on about all the things that had
been stolen. The silver tea service, the emerald
bracelet, the diamond brooch . . . Of course it was
absurd. They'd all have been sold long ago, but it
was as if she'd forgotten the years between and all
she could think of was that I should have had them,
that she should have been able to hand them on to
me.

"It's so clear in my memory. . . . Her lying there,
so—frail, the life in her petering out . . . desperately longing to give me a treasure, an heirloom.
And giving me this little old gray key! 'It's worth-
less,' she said. 'It's not even the proper one. . . .

It's Jessie's key, the one Jessie sent, that happened to fit . . . It's a skeleton key, it opens any lock. . . .' And she pressed it into my hand and whispered, 'My sweet girl, may it open doors for you, all your life. . . .' "

"What did you say?"

"I said, 'Does it open the jewel case?' and she said it did. So I said that the key and the jewel case were all the inheritance anyone could want."

Omri stopped dead in his tracks.

"What did you say?"

"I told her she could give me the jewel case. What was left of it . . . Of course it was a mess. The red leather was beginning to rot, the sides had come unglued, and the lid and the little trays were hanging off, but it was still a box, and it still had its key. And Granny Marie said, what was the use of an old empty box, and I said, but it's much more than that! It was given to her by Matthew on their honeymoon."

Omri could scarcely speak. He clutched her arm.

"But it was stolen," he managed to scrape out of a dry throat. "The burglar—stole it."

"Oh, yes, but didn't I tell you? The case was found afterward, thrown away in the garden. Of course, empty, but you know, she was so glad to at least have that back. She'd often told me the story of how an old Cockney lady who happened to be passing, and saw it under the front hedge,

brought it in to her a couple of days after the burglary, all muddy and bedraggled, and she hugged
it and cried over it, and forgot for the moment that
everything valuable had gone. It was a bit of Matt
for her to treasure."

Omri felt the sweet fresh air going down into
his lungs as he breathed deeply. Of course. *Of
course*. That was it—that was what he'd been trying to remember! His mother had told him—long
ago, when he'd first had the key—that the jewel
case had *fallen to pieces!* If she knew that, she must
have kept it until then. It must have been returned!

He was alive. He wasn't going to disappear, even
though Bert had kept his oath—to the letter. "I
will return the *jewel case*. . . ." And that was just
what he had done! The crafty little crook . . . And
who was the "old Cockney lady who happened to
be passing?" Could that have been Elsie? If it was,
and she'd rumbled Bert's trick, what would she have
done to him afterward? Would she really have
turned him in? He'd probably rather have faced the
cops than a furious Elsie—poor old Bert! Omri
suddenly began to laugh and cry at once.

"Omri! Darling, what is it?"

"Oh, Mum! It's okay, nothing, I'm okay, don't
mind me."

She was holding him tight. Gradually he calmed
down. He pulled away and wiped his nose on the
back of his hand.

"I don't fancy seeing the bison just now," he said. "Can we have an ice cream?"

They walked back to the big house with their arms around each other. Omri didn't feel there was anything childish about that at all. In fact, he felt extremely grown-up.

EPILOGUE

A Funeral— and After

None of the family felt called on to go to Tom Towsler's funeral with Omri a week later.

Patrick and Tony, of course, had gone home, and Omri and Gillon were back at school. Omri's mother had never met Tom, and his father—who might have gone simply out of respect—was being intensely busy doing-it-himself around the house and at the last minute said, "Could you do the honors by yourself, Omri? I'm just getting into this now, and it would mean putting on a suit." Omri's dad owned only one suit that had been going for ten years as he only wore it for weddings and funerals, which he grandly called "state functions."

So Omri took the morning off from school and

put on a suit himself (well, a pair of school trousers and a jacket and tie anyway), and cycled carefully to the village church. He purposely got there half an hour early.

He wasn't so eager for the funeral—who is?—but there was something he did want to do, and that was to find Jenny's grave.

Wandering around the churchyard, he tried to imagine where he would have put it if he'd been Tom, and he guessed somewhere quiet and private, and headed into the corners. Two yielded nothing, but in the angle of the third, protected by a straggly hedge, he found it.

It was beautiful and perfect, a work of love. The grave was six inches long, a neat oval mound covered, not with grass, but with a sweet-scented plant with tiny bright green leaves that Omri later found out was called chamomile.

There was a border of small, flat, white stones all around it to discourage the grass from overgrowing it too soon. The grass around it had been cut very short, perhaps with scissors, though it was growing out now. The cross was small to match the grave, but beautifully made of polished wood. It had a tiny plaque, about an inch square, made of a piece of brass, simply engraved:

Jenny
R.I.P.

Omri had no views about the hereafter. He didn't really think there was one. But a strange hope came to him as he crouched by the grave. He hoped that Tom had believed in one, one where time and size didn't matter, and people who had loved each other would come together.

"On my way, Jen . . ." Yes, Omri thought as he stood up and walked back to the front of the church. Tom had believed that he was going to find her.

After that, Omri didn't feel too sad at the funeral itself. But Peggy was in a bad way. She was sitting in the pew just in front of him (there were a lot of people in the church, including two of their own thatchers who nodded solemnly to Omri when they saw him) wearing dark clothes and a navy blue headscarf over her hair. She was crying all the way through the service. Omri felt really sorry for her, and after it was all over, he steeled himself to go up to her in the church porch, where she was standing near the vicar, accepting people's condolences.

When she saw him she grabbed him and gave him something like a hug.

"Thanks for comin'," she whispered in his ear. "I got somethin' he'd've wanted you to have. All them little plastic toys he kept so nice, his collection . . . You was the last one he talked to . . . Never woke up again after that." The memory seemed to affect her unbearably, and she burst into tears again and clutched Omri to her.

Feeling himself clasped in her arms, Omri moved a bit to free himself politely. By accident he brushed against the side of her head. The navy headscarf slipped, and he found himself staring at an aquamarine drop earring.

He cycled home in an unusual mood of philosophical acceptance.

Since he'd failed to find the earrings in the cashbox, he'd assumed Jessica Charlotte had sold them or hidden them somewhere. It never occurred to him that she had given them to Tom, as thanks for what he did for her at the end.

Well. So much for his hopes of handing them to his mother. He wondered if Peggy knew how valuable they were. Almost certainly not. Tom had called them "a trifle." Omri felt sad, a bit frustrated, but . . . well. There it was.

He asked himself if he would have traded the earrings for the sight of Jessica Charlotte singing. The chance of actually meeting her. The relief of knowing that he had not interfered—or rather, that the interference he'd intended hadn't changed anything. His gratitude to Patrick for being so unexpectedly sensible.

He decided he wouldn't. Those things were more important than earrings. He felt sorry his mother wouldn't have them, though. But then, when he thought about it, he decided she'd have looked funny in them. She only wore silver and fun stuff. Glittery real jewels weren't her style.

Well, that wrapped it all up. And speaking of wrapping up, he made up his mind that as soon as he got home, he'd wrap up the cupboard and get his dad to take it back to the bank. For good, this time. At least he'd resisted the temptation (reinforced by Patrick, who hadn't been too sensible to beg for just a brief chat with Boone) to bring their old friends to life.

Because there was no such thing, with this business, as a "brief chat." Bringing them back always led to something. Patrick had reluctantly seen the point in the end. He hadn't had the scare Omri had had, but he got the point just the same, and had taken Boone away with him, sadly but resignedly.

Omri leaned his bike against the front of the house.

Kitsa was playing with her kittens on the lawn. She'd brought them to show them off about three days ago, leading them in a line, tiny pointed tails erect, across the lane and up the path. The fuss that had been made of her mollified her (or possibly she just couldn't face lugging them all up that ladder again) and she had now taken up residence with her kittens in the bottom of a cupboard in one of the living rooms. As a direct result, the ground floor had become infested with fleas, the whole family was eaten alive, but nobody even thought of kicking her out or speaking a single cross word to her. She was queen of the house once again. (The pest man was coming today.)

Kitsa graciously allowed Omri to give her an admiring caress and even, briefly, to pick up one of the kittens to stroke. Then she put her front paws against his leg and administered a Kitsa-hint by sticking all ten claws into him. He laughed, put the kitten down, and went into the house.

"How was the funeral?" his mother called from the kitchen.

"Okay," said Omri.

"Surprise for you," she said. "Go and look in your bedroom and see what Dad's been doing!"

The first thing he noticed was that there were bolts on the insides of both the doors in his room.

"Oh, great, Dad, thanks!" he yelled, though there was no sign of his father now. Then he looked around again, and his blood congealed in his veins.

There was a series of properly fitted shelves at shoulder height on the wall. Prominently placed on one of them stood the cupboard, with the key in its lock.

Omri's arrangement of bricks and planks had gone.

He felt his legs buckle, and his face turn icy cold. He turned and stumbled out of the room and downstairs. He stood there at the bottom. He was afraid to his marrow, afraid to confront his father—afraid to ask.

His mother came past, and paused, seeing him so still.

"Anything wrong, love? Don't you like the shelves?"

He had to cough before he could speak. "Where—where did Dad put the—the bricks and stuff that were up there?"

"He was going to bash them up to make hardcore for a patio—"

Omri didn't listen to any more. He couldn't run, he felt too unsteady, so he walked, slowly and deliberately, down the path, through the gate, across the lane. . . . He found his father sitting in his studio. He wasn't working or painting. He wasn't doing anything, just sitting and staring out of the window.

"Dad."

He expected his father to turn to him the face people show when they expect to be thanked for something nice they've done. But he didn't look like that at all. He too looked as if he had had a shock. Omri knew at once that something fundamental had happened. A quantum leap.

"Dad? Where are they?" It seemed to take all his courage to frame the question.

"I put them where I thought they belonged," said his father in an odd voice.

They stared at each other for what seemed like a long time.

"Where?"

"In the cupboard, of course," his father said. "Isn't that where you put them?"

Another long silence. Then Omri forced himself again.

"Did you—you didn't lock them in?"

"Yes," said his father. "I locked them in."

Omri gave a gasp. "Then they're al—When?"

"About twenty minutes ago."

Omri turned to run. His father's voice stopped him.

"I heard them."

"What?"

"I heard them in there. I heard their voices."

He stood up shakily and came to the doorway where Omri was standing, tense in every muscle. He put his hand gently onto Omri's shoulder.

"It's true, isn't it," he said, in the voice of someone who only wants to be reassured that the world is still the world he woke up to in the morning. "Your story. It was all true."

Omri suddenly threw himself into his father's arms. Something long held in seemed to burst inside him. His father held him tightly, then held him away.

"Go on," he said. "Ask."

There was only one question that mattered.

"Have you told anyone?"

"Not a living soul. And furthermore, I am never going to."

Omri closed his eyes. Then he leaned forward, pressed his face once again against his father's shoulder, and turned and ran.

Safe—really safe, now—in his room, he slammed the bolts and flung himself at the cupboard. He could hear them now. Matron's voice, high-pitched, inquiring. Little Bear, answering in grunting tones. Fickits, barking orders. Only Bright Stars didn't seem to be talking, but there was a sudden wail as a baby started to cry. Mingled with it was the shrill whinney of a horse. Twenty minutes they'd been in there in the dark! Twenty minutes!

With infinite care, controling his rampaging excitement, Omri lifted the cupboard down and put it on his table. Then he turned the key and opened the door.

The horse braced its front legs and tugged at the rope, held in the hand of the Indian. Standing beside him was Bright Stars, holding a bawling year-old boy in her arms. When the light struck him, he stopped crying and stared, out of eyes like black olives, at Omri. His fat brown cheeks were streaked with tears and his black hair stood up on end.

Fickits wore a sergeant-major's stripes and had put on weight. He was red in the face, and his cap was on the ground. It appeared to have been jumped up and down on.

Matron's cap was well and truly on her head. It had reached new heights of importance, and her face matched it. She looked as if she was just dying to give whoever was responsible the telling-off of all time.

But it was at Little Bear that Omri principally looked.

He looked much as he had when Omri had first seen him. Bare-chested, with knife in hand, he stood, legs apart, looking ferocious and baffled.

But when he saw Omri, his face changed. It seemed to ignite.

"Hey, Little Bear!" Omri said.

"Brother!" shouted the Indian joyfully. He dropped the horse's rope and held out his hand. "This good! I have much need!"

"Why, what's wrong? Can I do something?"

Just at that moment, there was a tap on the door, and they all froze.

"Omri," said his father's soft voice. "May I come in?"

They all froze. Little Bear fixed Omri with a fierce grimace. He knew what an adult voice meant. Matron knew too—her hands flew to her mouth. Fickits sprang to attention, as if, whatever was about to happen, he was going to meet it like a true Royal Marine.

It was Bright Stars who spoke, in a terrified whisper.

"We hide? Omri tell what to do!" She had her hand over her baby's mouth—too tight! He looked as if he were about to burst.

There was another, gentle tap on the door.

Slowly, Ormi made himself relax.

"It's okay, Bright Stars," he said, keeping his voice steady to reassure them. "Let Tall Bear yell if he wants to."

Bright Stars tentatively removed her hand. Tall Bear's eyes bulged with rage. He drew a deep breath and gave the loudest bawl he was capable of.

Little Bear had to shout to make himself heard.

"Who big man voice, who make noise on wall?"

For answer, Omri went to the door, unbolted it, and stood aside.

Even Tall Bear, drawing breath for another howl, fell silent as a giant among giants walked into the room.

"This is my father," said Omri.

His father, with a look of absolute wonder on his face, came slowly forward, and then went down on his knees in front of the cupboard, bringing his face level with the little people. Bright Stars hid behind

Little Bear. Tall Bear's black eyes could be seen peering in awe over his father's bare shoulder. Matron's hands instinctively went up to straighten her cap. Fickits, his face a pale shade of putty, nevertheless managed a brief, convulsive salute.

"Dad," said Omri. "I'd like you to meet my friends."

There was a brief silence, and then his father said, "I am—incredibly—pleased—and honored—to meet you."

From now on, thought Omri, *whatever happens—and plenty will—Dad's in on it. Which is bound to make things . . . very, very complicated.*

But there was no room in his heart for anything but pleasure as they all gathered around to shake the giant's forefinger.